DI017596

# THE GEMINI MYSTERIES

## BOOK TWO
## THE CAT'S PAW

WITHDRAWN

## KAT SHEPHERD

YELLOW
JACKET

This book is for P-22,

and for the bits of wildness

that make their homes

in the hearts of all of us

–KS

 **YELLOW JACKET**

an imprint of Little Bee Books
New York, NY
Text copyright © 2021 by Kat Shepherd
Illustrations copyright © 2021 by Little Bee Books
Interior art by Damien Jones
All rights reserved, including the right of reproduction in whole or in part in any form.
Yellow Jacket and associated colophon are trademarks of Little Bee Books.
Manufactured in China RRD 0820
First Edition
1 3 5 7 9 10 8 6 4 2
Library of Congress Cataloging-in-Publication Data
Names: Shepherd, Kat, author.
Title: The cat's paw / by Kat Shepherd.
Description: New York, New York: Yellow Jacket, [2021]
Summary: Thirteen-year-old twins Zach and Evie and their friend Vishal
investigate the disappearance of Martin the red panda from the zoo, but is
the culprit a bobcat, animal activists, or exotic animal dealers?
Identifiers: LCCN 2019001786 | Subjects: | CYAC: Zoos—Fiction. |
Zoo animals—Fiction. | Twins—Fiction. | Brothers and sisters—Fiction. |
Friendship—Fiction. | Mystery and detective stories.
Classification: LCC PZ7.1.S514473 Cat 2019 | DDC [Fic]—dc23
LC record available at https://lccn.loc.gov/2019001786

ISBN
978-1-4998-0810-0 (hc)
978-1-4998-1037-0 (ebook)

yellowjacketreads.com

For more information about special discounts on bulk purchases, please
contact Little Bee Books at sales@littlebeebooks.com.

# CHAPTER
# 1

Evie Mamuya looked critically at her twin brother, Zach. He stood in front of her expectantly, his skinny arms jutting out awkwardly from his sides. "I don't know," she finally said. "It's hard to tell. Could you just act normal? You look like a scarecrow standing like that."

Zach sighed and dropped his arms. "Seriously? I've been standing here for like a hundred years, Evie. I just want to know if this is okay to wear to the dinner at the zoo tonight. Just say yes or no so we can both get on with our lives."

Evie narrowed her eyes at his pink button-down shirt and khaki pants, the pants a few shades paler than his light brown skin. "I don't know; I think you might need a tie."

Zach's eyes bulged. "A tie? Come on, Evie. We're going to the *zoo*." He folded his arms. "I'm not wearing a tie. That's dumb."

"Fine. Don't." Evie turned her back to him and fluffed her shoulder-length twist-outs as she looked in the mirror. She held up two different cardigan sweaters, seeing which matched better with the pineapple-print dress she was wearing. "But just remember, Sophia said this dinner was for *major donors*. Do you really want to be sitting at a table full of rich people and you're the only one not wearing a tie?"

Zach rolled his eyes and slouched out of the room. "You are so annoying," he muttered.

"Where are you going?" Evie asked.

"To put on a tie."

Evie smirked. The sharp sound of the front-door buzzer filled the apartment, and Evie heard her mom's voice drift back from the living room. "Vishal's on his way up!" Evie and Zach darted out of their rooms, almost colliding in the hall. Zach now sported a navy tie with a pattern of fluffy tan blobs.

Evie laughed. "OMG, are you really wearing your *hamster* tie?"

"It was the only one I could find!"

"Well, I think you look very handsome in it." Mrs. Mamuya stepped into the hallway and kissed the top of her son's head, her blue eyes warm. "I still remember buying you that tie for your ninth birthday. Do you remember?"

"Are you kidding? We *all* remember it. Hamsters were the only thing he talked about for our entire third-grade year!" Evie said. "I'm pretty sure he even wore that tie to soccer practice for a while."

"I did," Zach admitted.

"And here we are four years later and you're almost all grown-up." Mrs. Mamuya's smile was tinged with melancholy. "Your dad would be so proud if he could see you now." Evie and Zach leaned in for a family hug. Their father, Yaro, had died when the twins were three. Although they barely remembered him, they knew their mom still missed him.

Vishal Desai let himself in through the front door

and grinned at the knot of Mamuyas in the hallway. "Hey, Mam Fam."

The hug broke up, and Mrs. Mamuya gave Vishal a warm smile. "How's my second-favorite boy in the world?"

"I'm pretty excited about tonight," Vishal replied. He slouched effortlessly against the wall in a pair of dark pants and a pastel polo shirt, one hand tucked into the pocket of an unzipped charcoal hoodie. "The Boyds' car is already outside." He ran his free hand through his spiky hair and blinked at Zach. "Why are you wearing a tie?"

Zach turned to his mother and sister. "See? I told you. Vishal's not dressed up."

"I am too dressed up," Vishal said. "This is my best hoodie. It doesn't have a single hole in it!"

Mrs. Mamuya gently pushed her kids out the door. "Different families, different rules, Zach. Have fun, and don't forget to thank the Boyds for inviting you."

A large black SUV with tinted windows sat idling in front of the apartment. A man in a black suit and tie over a crisp, white shirt jumped out of the driver's seat and came around to open the back door. He grinned at the kids and tipped his black cap.

"Edgar!" Vishal's face lit up as he high-fived the chauffeur. Edgar was the Boyd family's driver, and he often ferried Sophia and her friends around town.

Vishal hopped into the front seat next to Edgar, and the twins joined Sophia in the back row of soft leather seats behind her parents. Dashiell and Mareva Boyd were both dressed elegantly but casually, Dashiell in a blue Oxford shirt and gray flannel pants, and Mareva in a black silk jumpsuit and espadrilles.

"Thank you so much for inviting us," Evie said. "I can't believe we get to go behind the scenes with some of the animals tonight!"

"It should be superfun," Sophia said confidently. "I heard some of the keepers talking about it." At Sophia's urging, her family had recently funded the zoo's brand-new gibbon exhibit, and Sophia spent every weekend volunteering as a junior zookeeper. She smiled at her friends. "You're gonna love it." Her head tilted to one side when she noticed Zach. "Why are you wearing a tie?"

"That's it. I'm getting rid of this stupid thing." Zach

yanked off the hamster tie and shoved it in his pocket.

The car turned from the main road and into the parkland that surrounded the city's zoo and botanical gardens. The sun hadn't set yet, but shadows were beginning to pool under the thick trees along the river. It was a warm spring night, and Evie opened her window. Flowers were starting to sprout on everything, and the first bright leaves of spring covered the trees in a mist of fresh green. It was a peaceful scene, but then Evie straightened in her seat with a cry. "You guys! Look!"

# CHAPTER

# 2

Evie pointed at the animal she had spotted through the trees. "What is that?"

Sophia shoved across the seat and squeezed in next to Evie. "Oh, my gosh! That's B-17! It's got to be!" She turned to her parents, eyes glowing. "Can you believe it? I never thought we'd be lucky enough to see her!"

"What's B-17?" Vishal asked, craning his neck to see across the car.

Sophia stretched her phone out the window in an effort to get a photo. "She's the wild bobcat that lives in the city. MEOWS has been studying her to learn more about how predators can adapt to new environments. I'm helping them plan a citywide festival this summer to raise awareness about her and other urban wildlife." She smiled down at the gray, blurry image on her screen. "I'm gonna tweet them right now to tell them about the sighting!"

Vishal cleared his throat. "I'm sorry, but did you just say MEOWS?"

Sophia looked at him flatly. "Yeah . . . why?"

Vishal snickered. "There's a group that studies bobcats, and it's called MEOWS?"

"Yes," Sophia said impatiently. "Minnesotans Empowering Our Wildlife Safety. What about it?"

"It's just, you know, MEOWS. Studying a cat? Don't you think that's kind of funny?" Vishal asked. Sophia stared at him. Zach and Evie shared a secret grin.

The group waved goodbye to Edgar at the zoo entrance, where there were several open trams lined up along the curb. There was an elderly couple already seated at the back of one of them. The man was thin and bent, and he wore a red, white, and blue sweatband stretched across his spotted, pink bald head. His wizened wife dug around in her huge purse, her elbow jabbing his ribs as she rummaged. Other couples milled about and chatted with docents in khaki-and-white uniforms. Nobody seemed to have any kids with them, and

Evie wondered if this was going to end up being one of those boring evenings where adults either ignored you or kept asking what you liked about school. She hoped it wasn't.

Then she spied someone she knew, and her face lit up. "Hey, look! It's Abby! Let's go say hi." Abigail Morris was a kindergarten teacher they had met a few months earlier, when she and her fiancé, Gideon Doheny, had gotten tangled up with the kids' last case. Evie still wasn't too sure about Gideon, but she liked Abby.

When the twins and their friends joined the group, Abby was standing a little bit to the side watching Gideon hold court with a cluster of people. "Abby!" Evie cried. "You'll never guess what we saw on the way over here!" She pulled Sophia over, and they showed off the blurry photo of B-17 to Abby's enthusiastic oohs and ahs.

Gideon pulled his fiancée out of the conversation to introduce her to another couple and a jolly-looking man with ivory hair and fat, rosy cheeks. Gideon noticed the children and smiled broadly, his gleaming teeth the exact same shade as his immaculate white suit. "Fancy meeting you here," he said with a condescending wink. "Tommy, let me introduce you to Sophia Boyd. She's Dashiell and Mareva's daughter." Tommy shook Sophia's hand vigorously. "And these are her little friends," Gideon added, without bothering to include their names.

Abby introduced Evie and the boys. The jolly man took Evie's hand in a crushing grip, shaking her arm like a dog with a rope toy. Evie noticed he wore a circular BIG TOMMY BROWN FOR MAYOR button on his lapel. He slapped both boys on the back, and Evie noticed her brother stumble a bit from the force of it. "Always a pleasure to meet such fine junior citizens. I'm City Councilman Tommy Brown, but most folks around here just call me Big Tommy," he said with a folksy grin. "It's nice to see you young people out and about and interested in something besides your phones." He laughed loudly at his joke, and it took everything Evie had not to roll her eyes. "Stay in school," he added, obviously finished with them, before turning back to the other couple with Gideon and Abby.

"I'll tell you what, Tommy, it's great to see you get the recognition you deserve for all the work you've done on behalf of the zoo over the years," Gideon said.

"Well, now, it sure was a surprise when the zoo called me a few months ago and said they wanted to honor me this evening," Tommy said with false modesty. "But it's been a treat to work side by side with them to plan this wonderful event and make sure that major donors like yourself have a really special time tonight."

"This is my new business partner, Dante Fishman, and his girlfriend, Bitsy Romanevsky," Gideon said.

"Of course!" Tommy said, slapping Dante on the back. "I'll tell you what, Dante, I've been hearing all about you from Darwin. Your generosity has made quite a difference to the zoo, which is why I insisted you be included in tonight's festivities."

"It's a pleasure to meet you, bro!" Evie watched in surprise as Dante grasped Tommy's hand and leaned in for a chest bump. Gideon's new business partner had curly dark hair and olive skin, and he was dressed like he had just wandered off a yacht. Evie could see bare ankles peeking out from between the hem of his duck-patterned pants and the shiny tops of his leather loafers. It was a warm evening, but his girlfriend, Bitsy, wore a luxurious red fox-fur jacket over her short dress, stroking it idly with her French-manicured fingers while she cast adoring glances at her boyfriend. A blond mane of hair, salon-perfect tan, and flashy designer handbag told Evie everything she needed to know about Bitsy, so Evie focused her attention back to Gideon.

"Dante's developing a new app that's going to sweep the casual gaming world by storm," Gideon said proudly, throwing his arm around Dante's shoulder.

Councilman Brown nudged Vishal with his elbow. "Uh-oh, sounds like something you boys are going to go crazy over with all your video gaming, am I right?" He guffawed.

Vishal shrugged politely. "I'm not really much of a gamer, actually. What's it called?"

"Monkeyfarts Mayhem," Dante said.

Vishal's eyes lit up. "Forget everything I just said. That sounds amazing!"

Zach chimed in. "Seriously. Do you need testers, because we will *totally* be testers for that!"

Everyone laughed except Sophia, who shook her head. "I still do not get what people think is so funny about"—she lowered her voice to a whisper—"*farts*."

Evie sighed. "Pretty much everything, Sophia. I don't really know how to break it down for you."

"Whatever," Sophia said dismissively. Leaving the boys behind with Dante, Sophia and Evie joined Sophia's parents, who were talking to a conservatively dressed man with high cheekbones and short-cropped salt-and-pepper hair.

Mareva reached out her hand to draw Evie into the conversation. "Evie, I'd like you to meet Dr. Darwin Chang. He's the zoo director. Our family worked closely with him on the gibbon exhibit, and he's become a good friend."

Dr. Chang shook Evie's hand, but his smile was tight and didn't spread to his eyes. He glanced quickly at his watch and gestured to the carts. "We're behind schedule; it's already six forty-seven. Shall we head into the zoo?" The docents ushered everyone on board.

The trams were just beginning to pull onto the path leading through the entrance when they were interrupted by an electronic screech. Evie spied the source of the noise across the parking lot. A young woman held a megaphone in one hand and a homemade sign in the other. She shouted something into the megaphone, but the sound was too garbled to understand what she was saying.

Sophia groaned in the seat next to Evie. "It figures *she* would be here."

"Who?" Evie asked.

"Jersey Sinclair. She's always in the parking lot, shouting at people." Sophia sounded irritated.

"What's she doing?" Evie asked.

"Protesting," Sophia answered. "She's an 'animal rights' person." Sophia made air quotes around the words *animal rights*.

The other guests craned their necks to see what the ruckus was about, and a few grumbled as they tried to read the green paint on her cardboard sign. Gideon made a loud joke at the woman's expense, and Abby looked down at her hands, which were twisted in her lap.

"Why would animal rights people protest a *zoo*?" Zach asked. He lowered his voice. "Do the keepers, like, mistreat the animals here or something?"

"Of course not," Sophia snapped. "Do you think I would volunteer here if they did?"

Sophia didn't speak for the rest of the ride, and Evie had an uneasy feeling as the trams wove through the unlit paths of the empty zoo. The sun was setting, and the animals they passed seemed wilder somehow in the quiet empty of the park. A tiger stood on its hind legs and stretched, raking its claws into the bark of a tree in its exhibit. Its powerful shoulder muscles rippled beneath striped fur as it cast a contemptuous glance at the carts driving by.

A few moments later a docent parked the cart near a warmly lit pavilion that overlooked the zoo's expansive elephant habitat. Evie could see the large barn in the distance, and a bull elephant slowly ambled through the tall grass over to a hay feeder near the pavilion's railing. Zach and Vishal ran over for a closer look, but Evie hung back for a moment to read the sign set up near the cloth-covered dining tables: TONIGHT'S DINNER HONORING LONGTIME FRIEND OF THE ZOO, COUNCILMAN TOMMY BROWN. There was a photo of the councilman from a previous zoo event, where he was grinning broadly and holding up a large boa constrictor, his round red face shiny with exertion.

Evie heard Vishal's excited cry. "Check it out, dude! He's just going for it!" Vishal pointed at the elephant that was using its trunk to insert an entire butternut squash in its mouth.

The old lady with the giant purse cackled next to him. "Oh, that's nothing! I've seen ole Billy here gulp down an entire watermelon like it was a jelly bean!"

Zach laughed and called to the girls. "Evie! Sophia! Come here! You gotta see this!"

"You guys go ahead. I'll be there in a sec," Sophia said to Evie. "I just want to show Dr. Chang my photo of B-17. Maybe I can get the zoo to offer to host the wildlife festival this summer." She looked up from her phone. "Where is Dr. Chang anyway? He was here a second ago."

# CHAPTER
# 3

Sophia pointed to the event sign. "There he is." She bit her lip. "I think I'll catch him later. He looks pretty mad right now."

Evie followed Sophia's finger. "Oh, wow. He sure does." Dr. Chang gesticulated angrily, his arms slicing the air to punctuate his point. His face was flushed. "I wonder who he's arguing with." The girls crept closer and hid behind a tree, trying to catch what the disagreement was about.

"What you are asking me to do is *illegal*," Dr. Chang hissed. "Not to mention completely unethical! I don't care how much money you're offering; I won't do it!" The other voice was muffled by the display, but Dr. Chang's reply was clear. "Don't you dare come into this zoo and threaten me. This conversation is *over*!" He turned abruptly on his heel and stalked back to the party.

Sophia and Evie exchanged a look. "Whoa," Evie said. "Intense. What do you think that was about?"

Sophia shook her head. "I don't know. Let's wait and see who else comes out." Sophia felt a hand on her shoulder, and she jumped, startled.

"There you are, girls," Mareva said. "The servers are bringing out the first course, and Dr. Chang said he would begin his speech promptly at seven fifteen, so we should find our table." She shepherded them back to the dining area, where everyone was taking their seats. Sophia tried to see who was missing, but there was too much movement to tell.

Zach and Vishal squeezed into their seats between the girls. "Thanks again for inviting us, Sophia," Zach said. "I can already tell it's going to be an unforgettable night."

\*\*\*

After the speeches, guests stood in clusters to have their pictures taken with Dr. Chang and Councilman Brown, who held up his Golden Gorilla Award proudly.

The award honored those who had made significant contributions to furthering the mission of the zoo, and Sophia hoped to win it someday. Just before the photographer snapped their picture together, Sophia snuck a peek at Dr. Chang. He was smiling confidently, and she would never have guessed he had lost his temper earlier if she hadn't seen it for herself.

After the dinner plates were taken away, the party broke into smaller groups. One gaggle of guests followed a guide to a cart and hopped on. Others chatted with zookeepers and docents who stood holding birds and other small animals. A tall, gray-haired docent with crinkly blue eyes and a name tag that said LANDES stood next to a wooden box with one open side.

Vishal pointed. "What's inside the box with that old wig?" The wig shifted slightly and stretched one long arm up to hook onto a wooden pole that extended across the box's inner walls. The hairy pile shifted some more, and a little face peered out of the long fur. "No way!" Vishal squealed. "It's so cute!"

"This is Prudence. She's a Linnaeus's two-toed sloth, and this is her nest box. It's one of her favorite places to hang out when she's in her enclosure." Landes held out a basket of rose blossoms. "Would you like to feed her?" The kids each took a blossom while Landes told them more about sloths and their habitats. Vishal held the rose blossom near Prudence's face, and she took it delicately, munching gently as her eyelids blinked and slowly started to close.

"Uh, is she okay?" Vishal asked.

Landes chuckled. "She might be dozing off. Sloths sleep a lot to conserve energy. Everything they do is slow. In fact, they don't ever leave their trees in the wild except to go to the bathroom, and they only do that about once a week."

Vishal gaped. "Wait a minute. Sloths only poop like once a week?"

Landes nodded. "The process of getting down the tree and to their favorite spot can sometimes take hours, so it can be quite dangerous. In fact, over half of all sloth deaths in the wild occur when they're—"

"Pooping!" Vishal crowed. He turned to Zach. "Dude! Where's that Dante guy? We have to tell him about this!"

Zach's eyes sparkled. "Right? That is, like, the best game idea ever! You're a sloth and you have to eat and move around, get down, poop, and get back up again without dying!"

"And then maybe you get extra points if the poop is like really big?"

"Yes!" Zach was almost hopping up and down with excitement. "And maybe eating different foods could give you special pooping powers and stuff!" He looked around. "We gotta find Dante!" But the app developer and his girlfriend were nowhere to be seen.

"They must be over at the rhino exhibit," Landes explained.

"The rhino exhibit?" Vishal asked.

Sophia clapped her hands. "Yes! I am so excited! Tonight, we get to go behind the scenes with Shakti, the zoo's Indian rhino! Isn't that amazing? We get to pet her and feed her apples!"

"Whoa," Zach said. "We get to . . . *pet* . . . a rhino?"

A green cart pulled up and guests filed out, still chattering excitedly about their experience. A waiting docent handed them gift bags, and they milled around, some pausing to grab a last drink or visit the animals. A dark-haired security guard with a long braid smiled as she directed the others toward the tram back to the parking lot.

Landes pointed at the cart. "Looks like we're the last group to go." Sophia ran over to get her parents, and everyone climbed aboard. Dr. Chang slipped into the front seat next to Landes, and the cart moved softly along the darkened path, stopping in front of a nearby barn where light streamed out from the open doorway.

Inside the barn, a keeper stood in front of a paddock fence that separated the building's corral and outdoor enclosure from the slop sinks, kitchenette, and hay storage. Just on the other side of the fence, a small gray mountain snuffled curiously at her hand. The mountain blinked her tiny eyes, and her pointed front lip wriggled in search of something to nibble.

"Welcome, everyone. I'm Roxanne, and this is Shakti, our Indian rhinoceros. She's a pretty special girl," the keeper said. "At forty-seven, she's officially the oldest rhino in captivity. And unofficially, that means she's the oldest rhino in the world that we know of."

"Cool," Evie said.

Roxanne ran her fingers lightly over a pinkish bump on top of Shakti's snout. "You might notice that Shakti doesn't have a horn. She was diagnosed with cancer in her horn a few years ago. We were able to remove it, and doctors from the University of Minnesota came right here to this barn to give her treatments, so she's been cancer-free for about two years now. As you can see, her horn is even starting to grow back." Roxanne patted the rhino's side and pointed to a cardboard box filled with apples. "Now, who wants to give her a snack?"

***

Zach was still asking Roxanne questions when he heard Evie calling his name. He looked over to find the rest of the group sitting in the cart, ready to go. Landes was gone, and Dr. Chang sat in the driver's seat and looked impatiently at his watch. "We gotta go, Zach," Evie called. "It's almost nine fifteen, and it was supposed to end at nine! Dr. Chang's gonna take us straight to the parking lot."

"Sorry," Zach said. "I'll be right there." He thanked Roxanne and gave Shakti a final goodbye pet, stroking the velvety soft skin beneath the folds of her thick hide.

He leaned forward and gave her a gentle peck on her side before scampering back to the cart.

"Dude, did you just kiss a rhino?" Vishal asked.

"So what?" Zach said. "Shakti's awesome. I was scared at first, because I thought rhinos were supposed to be all tough and dangerous, but she was more like a big golden retriever or something."

"In many ways the Indian rhinoceros is a gentle giant, but it can certainly be dangerous if it feels threatened or needs to defend its territory. Part of what makes Shakti so special is how comfortable she feels around people. Of course, she's still a wild animal, and at 3,500 pounds, she could easily hurt someone even by accident. It's important for all our keepers and guests to follow protocols like protected contact," Dr. Chang said.

"That's why she was behind a fence," Sophia explained.

"Too bad," Vishal teased. "Otherwise, Zach would probably have spooned with her." Zach laughed and punched Vishal's arm.

"Better look out, Vish," Evie said. "Zach might have a new BFF."

"Yeah, dude," Zach said. "You've been replaced."

"Never." Vishal smirked and folded his arms.

Just then the cart's radio crackled to life, and Dr. Chang snatched it up. "Could you repeat?" The garbled voice spewed forth a series of numerical codes. "Copy that." The zoo director's voice was clipped. "Get the lights set up and ready to go."

Evie leaned over to Zach and spoke softly in his ear. "What's going on?"

"I don't know," Zach answered, "but it looks like we aren't headed home anytime soon."

# CHAPTER
# 4

Dr. Chang turned away from the exit and drove farther into the darkness of the empty zoo. Everyone in the group was silent and tense, and Vishal could just make out the menacing silhouettes of the nocturnal animals prowling their exhibits as the electric cart sped toward its unknown destination. There was a ghostly roar as they passed a roundhouse, and Vishal jumped. "What was that?!"

Dr. Chang said nothing. He gripped the steering wheel tightly, the knuckles of his golden-brown hands pale with tension. Sophia glanced at him and shifted nervously in her seat. "I think it's probably a black howler monkey."

"That's a *monkey*?" Zach whispered. "It sounds like a dragon!"

"That's a much cooler description than what I would have come up with," Evie said.

"What do you think it sounds like?" Sophia asked.

"Someone burping into a microphone."

Dr. Chang pulled the cart in front of a high-walled open-air exhibit that was sunken below the path and surrounded by a dry, narrow moat. He jumped out and joined the cluster of staff who were huddled together over the zoo map. Maintenance workers adjusted tall, portable floodlights, directing the beams into the exhibit and the surrounding area. Keepers scoured the hard, dry-packed earth and shone flashlights into the branches of the exhibit's trees and climbing structures.

"Oh, no." Sophia and the others climbed out of the cart. "It's Marvin. Is he missing?"

Dashiell Boyd put a sympathetic hand on his daughter's shoulder. "It looks like it, Soph. But don't worry; I'm sure they'll find him. Your mom and I will go see what we can do to help."

Vishal cringed. "Are you telling me there's an escaped animal somewhere?" He backed away, bumping into a tree and rattling the branches overhead. His eyes darted to the source of the sound. "What was that?!" A blossom fluttered down from the tree and landed on his shoulder. He screamed and slapped at himself. "Something's touching me! Get it off! Get it off!"

"Relax, dude; it's only a flower." Zach held up the delicate pink bloom. "See?"

"Sorry." Vishal looked sheepish. "I just really don't want to get eaten."

Sophia's voice was scathing. "I'm pretty sure you're safe, Vishal. Marvin's a red panda."

"Pandas are no joke," Vishal said. "I've seen the panda attack videos! There's one where this panda grabs a guy and rips his coat off!"

Sophia sighed and pulled up a picture on her phone. "*This* is a red panda."

Vishal's voice went high when he saw the photo of a furry red animal that was only slightly bigger than a house cat. "Aww, it's so cute, like a little fox bear with a raccoon tail!" He passed the phone to Evie and Zach.

"Don't you just want to boop its little nose so bad?"

Evie nodded. "Totally. That is a face with a super-boopable nose." She returned Sophia's phone. "I hope they find him soon. Has he ever gotten out before?"

Sophia shook her head. "The exhibit was designed for him. He shouldn't be able to get out unless a keeper left a door open or something." She gestured to a uniformed zookeeper who was meticulously combing through the exhibit, pausing every so often to talk into a radio. "But Nikki's been working with Marvin since the zoo rescued him. I can't imagine her making a mistake like that."

Zach eyed one of the taller trees in the open-air enclosure. "Maybe one of the branches got too long and he was able to climb out that way?"

The others shrugged. "Maybe," Evie said.

Just then, there was a cry from Marvin's enclosure. Nikki's flashlight illuminated something in the wet sand near Marvin's drinking pool, and the other staff members crowded around to see, blocking the kids' view from above.

Dr. Chang shook his head grimly and left the group to speak into the ear of one of the security guards. She had a long, dark braid, and Evie recognized her from the party earlier. She conferred briefly with the Boyds before striding briskly over to where the kids were trying to peer into the exhibit. The rest of the staff started to disperse, their faces worried and sad.

The guard smiled apologetically. Her name tag read KRISTIN TONGSON, and she had a large ring of keys clipped to the belt of her uniform. "Sorry about the detour. Dr. Chang asked me to give you a lift back to your car."

"What did they find inside the exhibit?" Sophia asked anxiously. "Is Marvin okay?"

"It's too soon to know anything yet," Officer Tongson said, her expression noncommittal. She gestured to the nearby cart where Sophia's parents sat, talking quietly to each other. "Your gift bags are waiting for you at the zoo entrance, so don't forget to grab them on your way to your car."

Dashiell and Mareva huddled closer together, and Dashiell patted the seat beside him. "Here, Sophie Bear.

Why don't you squeeze in with us?" he said.

Sophia froze and narrowed her eyes suspiciously. "Why? What's wrong?"

Mareva's eyes widened in an expression of innocence. "There's nothing wrong."

"Yes, there is," Sophia said. "You guys haven't called me Sophie Bear since I was little except when there's something wrong, like when you told me Grandpa Boyd had cancer."

Dashiell chuckled uncomfortably. "I guess you all don't call yourselves the Gemini Detective Agency for nothing." His voice softened. "Why don't we talk about it in the car?"

Sophia put her hands on her hips. "No. I'm not a baby, you guys. If there's something bad you need to tell me, I'd rather hear it now."

"I think I know what it is," Zach said quietly. He pointed into Marvin's empty enclosure.

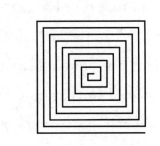

# CHAPTER
# 5

Vishal and the twins rode their bikes to Sophia's house the next morning. When the keeper's flashlight had illuminated a bobcat paw print in Marvin's exhibit the night before, it seemed to confirm everyone's worst fears: that the adorable little panda had become a hungry bobcat's dinner. Sophia had been pale and quiet during the car ride home, and her friends were worried about her. Sophia spent almost all her free time at the zoo, and they knew she had grown attached to most of the animals there.

Evie wheeled her bike to the edge of the driveway and tapped the kickstand. "I hope she's okay." She took off her neon-green helmet and rested it on the handlebars. "Remember how upset she was when Ben the spider monkey died of old age? She still can't talk about him without crying."

"I know," Zach said somberly. "She keeps a framed photo of him in her locker next to a red heart magnet that says 'Miss U.' It makes me so sad whenever I see it." He leaned his bike against a tree and hooked his yellow helmet's chin strap carefully around the seat.

Vishal dumped his dirt-covered bike unceremoniously on the ground and dropped his helmet on the grass next to it. "And then knowing that Marvin probably got eaten by that wild bobcat she loves?" He shuddered. "That is, like, therapy-level stuff." He jumped up to touch a low-hanging branch. "So. Many. Feelings."

The Sophia who greeted them at the door wasn't the swollen-eyed, tearstained girl they were expecting. Instead she looked fresh-faced and composed, every brunette hair of her sleek, blunt-cut bob perfectly in place. "Oh, hey. Glad you guys are here. Come on in." Her friends looked at one another in surprise and followed her up the curving grand staircase and along the wide upstairs hallway to her room.

"You seem like you're in a good mood," Zach said carefully.

"Why wouldn't I be?" Sophia asked.

"Well, I don't know. . . . I guess we thought you might be upset after last night. You know, like with what happened with Marvin and B-17 and everything."

Sophia flopped down on the white canopy bed in the middle of the room. "Oh, that's old news."

"What are you talking about?" Evie asked, sinking into a pink velvet armchair. "It happened just last night." Zach and Vishal sprawled onto the matching sofa, and Vishal immediately kicked off his shoes and stretched out his long legs onto a furry, blush-pink ottoman.

Sophia pulled a gold-colored laptop out from under a pile of throw pillows on her bed. "Well, yeah, I was pretty upset at first, but then I started researching, and you'll never guess what I found. Check this out." She tapped a few keys and pulled up an article to show them. "Did you know that red pandas are amazing escape artists? A red panda named Rusty escaped from his exhibit in 2013, and they found him hiding in a bush a day later. I'm sure Marvin just did the same thing." She nodded confidently. "I bet they'll find him really soon."

Zach and Evie looked at each other. "But," Evie said hesitantly, "what about the paw print? What about B-17?"

Sophia shook her head. "I don't think it was her. She's only ever eaten rabbits."

"Okay," Zach said. "But we did see her near the zoo last night."

Sophia sighed, exasperated. "She was only *exploring*. Her paw print was right by the water pool, right? She probably popped into Marvin's enclosure for a quick drink of water, and that got him all freaked out so he escaped. I mean, why would she eat him?"

"Uh, she's a bobcat," Vishal said. "She'll eat anything. I'm pretty sure she'd eat *me* if she had the chance."

"Whatever," Sophia scoffed. "You think *every* animal would eat you."

"No, I don't," Vishal said defensively.

Zach laughed. "Dude. Last night you were scared of a *flower*!" Evie and Sophia cracked up, and the tips of Vishal's ears turned pink.

"Look, B-17 wouldn't eat Marvin, okay?" declared Sophia. "If you don't believe me, we can go to MEOWS right now and ask them." She closed her laptop and bent down to pull on a pair of expensive suede slip-on sneakers. "In the whole time they've been studying her, she's basically eaten nothing but wild rabbits like ninety-nine percent of the time."

"What about the other one percent?" Zach asked, standing up.

"Mostly rats, mice, stuff like that."

"Yeah, but how do they know?" Evie challenged.

"By studying her scat," Sophia said, like it was the most obvious thing in the world.

"Yeah, sure. Of course." Vishal slipped on his scuffed shell toe sneakers. "What's scat?"

Sophia looked uncomfortable. "It's, well . . . you know"—she lowered her voice—"poop."

Zach and Vishal burst out laughing, and Evie grinned. "Wait, what?!" Vishal cried. "There are seriously scientists who look at *poop*?"

"Oh, get over it, Vishal. It's obviously not all they do," Sophia huffed.

"But still," Zach said. "That's like their job? They get paid for it?"

"Scat shows them important stuff, like what the

animals eat and when, and whether they're healthy. I don't see why you have to act like it's such a big deal." Sophia snatched up her cell phone. "Come on. Edgar can drive us."

Zach struggled to keep a straight face. "Oh, no, you're right. Definitely not a big deal. By all means, let's have Edgar drive us to meet with the poop scientists." Vishal's high-pitched giggle built to a frenzy, and he curled into himself like a question mark.

"Oh, grow up." Sophia sashayed past them, chin held high, and sucked her teeth in disgust. "Boys are so immature, aren't they, Evie? Let's go. MEOWS is expecting us."

"Yeah, guys, totally immature," Evie said. "Now, hurry up. You don't want to keep the poop scientists waiting, do you?"

Sophia walked stiffly down the hallway, with Evie's and the boys' ringing laughter following behind.

***

MEOWS was located in the basement of a small office building near the university. Two people bent over a large computer monitor looked up and greeted Sophia warmly. "Guys, this is Maggie," Sophia gestured to a young woman with light brown skin and glossy raven hair framing a heart-shaped face. "And this is Eric." Eric was slight, with pale skin and gray eyes that blinked behind wire-rimmed glasses. Both were dressed casually in T-shirts and jeans.

Evie leaned over and whispered in Sophia's ear. "Where are the scientists?" Her words sounded loud in the tiny room.

"Actually, that would be us," Eric said.

Evie looked embarrassed. "Oh, sorry. For some reason I thought you'd be wearing white coats and goggles or something, but I guess that's just on TV."

Maggie laughed. "If we're working on something in the lab we might, but most of the time we just wear our regular clothes."

"Where's the lab?" Zach looked around the cramped little room, with its messy desks and walls covered with charts, maps, and nature photographs.

"It's over at the U," Maggie explained. "Eric and I are graduate students. We work here part-time, and the rest of the time we're at school."

"B-17 is actually part of our PhD project," Eric explained. "Maggie and I darted her last summer, and while she was knocked out we were able to fit her with a radio tracking collar. It's been a great way to learn more about her movements." He turned the monitor to face the kids. "See? The GPS on her collar sends a signal every three hours to tell us where she is. These connected dots on the electronic map show where B-17 has been, and if you hover the mouse over a dot, it gives you the three-hour window of when she was there."

Zach bent over for a closer look. "Huh. It looks like she spends a lot of time near the river."

Vishal grimaced. "Remind me to stay away from the river."

Eric smiled. "B-17 doesn't pose any real danger to humans. Bobcats are actually pretty shy of people. In fact, most people never even know that they're there."

"That's not a very comforting thought," Vishal said.

"One of the things we're studying is how wild predators and humans can live together safely," Maggie said. "After all, as their habitats continue to shrink and disappear, animals like bobcats have to learn to adapt to us in order to survive, and we have to learn to adapt to them."

Eric pulled up a spreadsheet on another monitor. "From dissecting her scat"—at the word *scat*, Vishal and the twins exchanged knowing smirks, and Sophia studiously ignored them—"we've found that B-17's diet primarily consists of rabbits, small rodents, and birds. While some bobcats have been known to kill and eat deer, B-17 hasn't, or at least not since we've been studying her."

"So you don't think she ate Marvin?" Zach asked.

Maggie shrugged. "We can't say for sure that she wouldn't, but venturing into the zoo and attacking an animal isn't something she's ever done before."

"Did she go into the zoo last night?" Evie asked.

Maggie pointed back to the dots on the screen. "This dot here is time-stamped at seven fifteen last night, and it shows her in the arboretum near the zoo."

"That's not long after we saw her," Sophia said.

Evie opened up a zoo map. "But did she go into the

zoo? Did she go near Marvin's exhibit?"

"We don't know," Eric said. "The collar's GPS only sends a signal once every three hours, so the next blip wasn't until about ten fifteen."

"Where was she at ten fifteen?" Zach asked.

"She had moved to some neighboring parkland, in this region right here." Eric pointed at another dot on the screen. "There's a lot of thick forest over there, and several lakes. Good habitat for her."

"She could have gone anywhere in those three hours," Vishal said. "We can't prove she wasn't in the zoo." He reached down and fiddled with the zoo map as he thought, folding and unfolding it.

"But we also can't prove that she *was*," Sophia said. "And you heard Maggie and Eric. She's never done anything like this before. Why would she now? It's not like she doesn't have a steady supply of wild rabbits to eat."

"Yeah, but don't forget there was that bobcat print inside Marvin's exhibit," Evie said. Sophia's expression darkened, and she folded her arms.

"Could it be a different bobcat?" Zach asked. "Maybe one that you aren't tracking?"

"If so, it wouldn't be a female," Maggie explained. "Female bobcats never have overlapping territories. The only wildcat willing to get this close to B-17 would be a male during mating season, but that's in late winter. Since it's already May, any interested males would be long gone by now."

"So I guess we're back to B-17," Evie said. "For whatever mysterious reason, she must have gone hunting in Marvin's enclosure."

"If that's true, then it would have to be a really good reason to bring her in there," Vishal said, pointing at the zoo map.

# CLUE

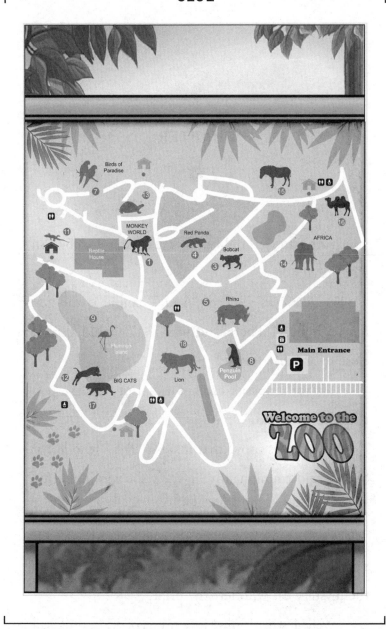

49

# CHAPTER
## 6

"Marvin's exhibit is right next to Thandie's exhibit, isn't it?" Vishal asked.

Sophia's eyes glowed. "And Thandie is the zoo's female bobcat! There's no way B-17 would get that close to another female!"

"That still doesn't explain the print near the pool, though," Evie said.

"But it does prove that it wasn't B-17 who left it," Sophia said triumphantly. "I knew she was innocent!"

"Then what *did* happen to Marvin?" Zach asked.

"I still think it was another bobcat: Mr. X," Evie said. The others looked at her. "That's what I'm calling the mystery cat who left the print."

"Well, I still think Marvin escaped," Sophia said.

"Let's go to the zoo and talk to Nikki. Maybe she found some more clues since last night."

The group said goodbye to Maggie and Eric and headed outside to where Edgar was waiting in the black SUV.

A short time later, the four teens knocked on a heavy green door behind Marvin's exhibit. The door was opened by a short, muscular woman with blond pixie-cut hair and a baseball cap pulled down over swollen, red-rimmed blue eyes. She gave a watery smile when she saw Sophia. "Hey, girl. How's our favorite volunteer?"

Sophia gave her a hug and introduced her friends. "Guys, this is Nikki Savoian. She's Marvin and Thandie's keeper, and she also takes care of some other animals in this part of the zoo." She turned to Nikki. "How are you doing?"

Nikki let out a heavy sigh. "I'm having a pretty rough time, to tell you the truth. I'd be lying if I said I haven't spent half the morning crying. Marvin was orphaned by poachers; he was only a baby when he came to the zoo, and I hand-raised him. He was still a wild animal, of course, but we were pretty bonded.

He would come over to me whenever I entered his enclosure, and take food right out of my hand. Such a sweet, lovable, dopey little guy." She shook her head. "It breaks my heart to lose him like this."

"So you think for sure he was killed by a bobcat?" Zach asked.

"I don't see what else could have happened," Nikki answered. "We found that track in the mud, and there's no way Marvin could have escaped on his own."

"Are you certain?" Sophia asked. "I read that red pandas are pretty amazing at getting out of their exhibits."

"Here," Nikki said. "I'll show you." They followed her through the little kitchen and storage building behind the enclosure and waited as she unlocked a metal door that led to a small, concrete vestibule. There was another heavy door in front of them, and chain-link gates to their left and right, each securing a small indoor enclosure with a heat lamp, climbing structures, and cozy perching platforms piled with shavings and old blankets. "This was Marvin's indoor space; he could come in here if it was too cold outside, the weather was crummy, or it got too hot. Red pandas don't tolerate heat well, so these are air-conditioned in the summer." She yanked a chain on a pulley, and up slid a small metal flap near one of the platforms.

"Oh, cool, it's like a little doggy door," Zach said.

"Unless we needed to keep Marvin contained for some reason, we generally leave these sliders open, and he could come and go as he pleased," Nikki said, "When I last checked on him yesterday evening right before the event, he was curled up in his nest box outside." Nikki used her set of keys to unlock the second door, and the kids followed her into the outdoor exhibit.

Vishal prowled the exhibit, lightly touching the trees and climbing structures that filled it. "Wow. I've been in a zoo before, but I've never really been *in* a zoo, if you know what I mean." He pointed up past the high concrete wall to the walkway above. "So that's where we were standing last night, right?"

Nikki nodded. "The enclosure is sunken like this so it can have high walls and the public can still see in. It's similar to the big cat exhibits you see in a lot of zoos."

Sophia ran her hand along the smooth concrete

walls. "And Marvin couldn't scale these?"

"His claws were pretty sharp, but not *that* sharp." She pointed to a line of wire several feet below the wall's lip. "And we also have electrified wire set up just in case."

"But wouldn't the wire have kept a bobcat out, too?" Sophia asked.

"It's supposed to," Nikki answered, "but cats are quite a bit more agile than red pandas, so it's hard to know for sure."

"And he couldn't have gotten out through the building?" Sophia asked carefully.

"Believe me, it's the first thing I thought of," Nikki said. "But I always double-check my doors, and I always note it on a clipboard whenever I enter the exhibit." She opened the inside door and grabbed a clipboard that hung from a nail on the vestibule wall. She pointed to the recent entries, dated and timed from the night before. "One of the other keepers had to help prep for the event last night, so I took care of the animals on her string before I finished up with mine. I didn't get to Marvin's enclosure until 7:32 p.m., when I gave him his dinner and his vitamin supplements." She pointed to two timed and dated boxes at the end of the line, both checked off. "The first mark confirms that the door was locked before I entered the exhibit, and I ticked the second one off after I left the exhibit and locked the door behind me." She pointed to the lower part of the page with handwritten notes. "I noted here that he was lethargic and didn't seem very interested in his dinner yet, so that's why I came back to look in on him again after the event. I was worried he might be ill. But instead he was gone."

Sophia tried to hide her disappointment. "So it seems pretty unlikely that he could get out?"

Nikki's eyes grew wet. "Believe me, I would give anything to find out that Marvin had gotten out, because it would mean that we could find him again and bring him home." She shrugged helplessly. "But I know Marvin, and I just don't think he would have been able to escape, even if he'd wanted to." She blinked away tears and sighed as she bent down to pick up a few stray bits of debris that littered the sand floor of the exhibit. The kids could hear the forced lightness in her voice as she changed the subject. "This is one of the downsides of an exhibit like this. I'm always having to pick up trash that ends up in here. I don't know whether it gets dropped by accident or on purpose, but every time I look, there's always more."

"We can help you clean up," Sophia said.

"Thanks," Nikki said. "We used to have more groundskeepers to help out, but ever since the most recent round of budget cuts, we've had to do more and more on our own."

Evie picked up a few wrappers and an empty water bottle. "Wow, is that all from today?"

"Some of it could be from yesterday. I had to help the staff prep the education animals for the dinner last night, so I was planning to clean and rake Marvin's exhibit when I came back. When I discovered that he was missing, cleaning the enclosure was the last thing on my mind."

"When did you realize he was gone?"

"At about nine fifteen. I always check the animals on my string before I leave for the night, to make sure everyone's healthy and where they should be." She bent over and grabbed a crumpled brown paper napkin near the wall.

Vishal picked up an empty Tupperware container. "This doesn't look like trash. Do you keep Marvin's food in here or something?"

Nikki inspected it. "I do keep treats for him in plastic containers, but this isn't the brand I use." She sniffed the inside. "And this smells like raw meat. Marvin is technically a carnivore, but a red panda's diet is almost exclusively bamboo. I've seen him catch an occasional bird or squirrel in his exhibit sometimes, but we don't feed him meat as a part of his regular diet." She handed it back to Vishal. "Someone must have dropped it in here by accident."

The kids followed her back into the building to throw the trash away. "Thanks for helping out today," Nikki said.

"If you ever need us to come again, we'd be happy to," Evie said. "It's kind of fun picking up the trash and knowing that we're keeping the animals safe.

Nikki walked the group back out to the front of the exhibit. "Well, believe me, it is always appreciated." She pointed to the litter on the ground outside the exhibit's wall. "There's a reason I work with animals instead of people. I mean, the trash can is right over there. Why can't people just use it?"

"Hang on a sec," Sophia said. "Can you take me back inside again? There's something I need to get."

# CHAPTER

# 7

Sophia emerged from the red panda building a few moments later, carrying the plastic container that Vishal had found. She waved goodbye to Nikki and returned to her friends. "What's with that?" Vishal asked, gesturing to the container.

Sophia pointed at the litter on the ground outside the exhibit. "See that 'FREE MARVIN' pamphlet? I think I know who left it, and I think this Tupperware was part of their scheme! Come on!"

Sophia's mouth was set in a grim line, and she strode purposefully toward the zoo's exit, the others trotting to keep up with her. "Where are we going?" Zach asked.

"To catch a thief," Sophia answered.

Back at the zoo entrance, Sophia jabbed an accusing

finger to where Jersey Sinclair stood pushing pamphlets at passersby. "I'll bet you anything Jersey left those pamphlets by Marvin's enclosure. And if she wants to free him that badly, what's to stop her from kidnapping him herself?"

The others looked thoughtfully at the activist. Her dirty blond hair was piled in a messy bun on top of her head, and she wore a bright-green tank top and a long, wrinkled peasant skirt. Her arms were tattooed and wiry, and her feet were shoved into scuffed rubber clogs. When a man refused to take a flyer from her, she picked up her electronic megaphone and shouted something into it, making him jump.

"That does make a lot of sense," Zach said. He turned to the others. "What do you guys think?"

Vishal nodded slowly. "She could have used that container of meat to lure Marvin into a carrier or something, and then she could have taken him away somewhere."

"Definitely," Evie agreed. "Nikki did say that he always came over to her in the enclosure. He was probably so used to being around people that I bet he would go up to anyone who went in there with food."

"Okay," Zach said. He closed his eyes, thinking. "So we've got good reason to think Jersey could have taken Marvin." He ticked off the reasons on his fingers. "She had motive, she had opportunity, and we have evidence to suggest she was at the scene of the crime. Now we just need a plan. I would vote against confronting her until we get more evidence. What do you think, guys?" There was no answer. "Guys?" Zach opened his eyes to find he was standing alone. Sophia was already marching toward Jersey shooting daggers with her eyes, and Evie and Vishal looked equally ready for confrontation. "Why do they always do this?" he moaned, hurrying after them.

When Zach finally reached the group, things did not seem to be going well. Sophia's face was white with anger, and Jersey had her arms folded and a smirk on her face. "Well, if it isn't the little princess," Jersey sneered. "What's wrong? Did you run out of Mommy's diamonds to sell so you could build more animal prisons?"

*Oh, boy,* Zach thought, bracing himself.

"How DARE you!" Sophia flew at the young woman.

Evie grabbed Sophia's arm and pulled her back. "Take it easy. Don't let her get to you."

"For your information, we weren't just building a habitat for *critically endangered* gibbons; the zoo also supports programs that help to protect gibbons in the wild. But obviously you don't care about that!" Sophia's voice was shaking. "You know, I want to help animals just as much as you do, but for people like you it's never good enough! At least I'm actually *doing* something about it, instead of just standing here shouting at people!"

Zach quietly cleared his throat. "Um, Sophia, you actually kind of are standing here shouting at people." He cleared his throat again. "I mean, at least right now."

"Whatever," Sophia huffed. She held up the bright-green FREE MARVIN flyer and shook it in Jersey's face. "You know, I thought there was no stunt you wouldn't pull, but you've really outdone yourself this time!"

Jersey laughed. "Oh, did I finally get your attention?"

"So you admit it?" Sophia demanded.

"Well, duh," Jersey said. "My organization's listed right there." She pointed at the black lettering on the bottom edge of the flyer: *For more information, contact SCAT!*

Vishal punched Zach in the arm. "Dude, does that say *scat*?" he whispered. They both cracked up, and Evie bit her lip to hide her smile.

"What about it?" Jersey snapped. "SCAT stands for Save Captive Animals Today. Why would that be funny?"

"I mean, scat, you know, like, animal scat, as in . . . " Vishal trailed off as he noticed both Sophia and Jersey glaring at him with identical death stares. "Never mind," he mumbled. "Just go back to yelling at each other."

Sophia stood arms akimbo. "So you're saying that all of this was just a publicity stunt for SCAT?"

Vishal giggled behind her, and Evie kicked his ankle. "Sorry," he whispered.

"It's not a *publicity stunt*," Jersey shot back. "It's an *awareness-raising campaign*. People need to know that innocent animals are being kept in prisons when they should be free. Imagine if you were just taken from your home one day and forced to live in a cage the rest of your life. Marvin belongs in the wild, not locked behind bars. All animals do!"

"First of all, Marvin wasn't taken from his home. He was orphaned by poachers, and he would have died if a zoo hadn't taken him in and nursed him back to health. The zoo *is* his home!" Sophia moved forward so she was almost nose to nose with the activist. "And second of all, Marvin wouldn't even know how to survive in the wild, so the sooner you tell us where you took him, the better."

Jersey stared at Sophia, dumbstruck. "What are you talking about?"

"Oh, don't play dumb now," Sophia said. "You've already admitted to kidnapping Marvin."

Jersey paled. "Wait, what? No, I didn't. Are you saying Marvin's *missing*?" She looked genuinely shocked, and Evie stepped in before Sophia could respond.

"He went missing from his enclosure last night.

Didn't you see it in the news?"

Jersey waved a hand dismissively. "Oh, I don't follow the news. It bums me out too much." Her face grew serious again. "But he's definitely gone? He must have escaped! See, he's been longing to be free all this time. I knew it! That's why I left those leaflets in the zoo, so that the people would finally come to know his plight."

"Marvin didn't escape," Zach said. He held up the plastic container from his exhibit. "Someone took him."

"Not just someone." Sophia pointed at Jersey. "*She* took him."

"Listen," Jersey said. "That poor animal finally escaped from your precious zoo, and you want someone to blame? Well, don't go looking at me. I'm not about to get framed for something I had nothing to do with."

"From our perspective, it looks like you had something to do with it," Zach said. He pointed to the flyer. "We saw you outside the zoo last night, and you've already told us you left those flyers near Marvin's exhibit. You could easily have snuck into the zoo and used Marvin's favorite treats to lure him away."

"Killer idea, kid, but it's not happening." Jersey brushed a stray strand of stringy hair away from her face. "Yeah, I left the leaflets yesterday afternoon. And yeah, I want Marvin to be free, but I'm not stupid. I'm not going to just grab an animal and randomly let it go somewhere that's nothing like its natural habitat. Marvin is a red panda. He belongs in the Himalayas, not Minnesota."

Sophia folded her arms and shot Jersey a skeptical glare. "Oh, so now all of the sudden you have a conscience?"

"I don't have any trouble sleeping at night," Jersey retorted. "Do you?" She saw the expression on Sophia's face, and she sighed. Her tone softened. "Look, you're obviously really worried about the little guy. And to be honest, I am, too. But I'm telling you, I didn't take him."

"What about this?" Zach held up the plastic container. "It was only a couple feet away from the leaflets you left. Maybe you wouldn't set Marvin free here, but that doesn't mean you wouldn't keep him for a while until you could send him somewhere else."

Jersey shook her head. "I don't know anything about taking care of a red panda, and I don't want to. SCAT doesn't even believe in owning pets." She took the empty meat container from Zach's hand and gave it a sniff. Her lip curled in distaste, and she quickly shoved it back to him. "And even if I did want to free him, I would never do it with *this*."

# CHAPTER
## 8

"I'm a vegan, guys. No animal products of any kind, and *definitely* no meat. Do you really think I would advocate the murder of one animal just to free another one from prison?"

"Whoa. Okay," Evie said. She chose her next words carefully. "You obviously have strong beliefs. But couldn't that mean you would be willing to sacrifice *anything* for your cause? Even if that means, um, you know, using meat?"

"Exactly," Sophia added. "Right now we just have your word, and why should we trust that?"

"Look, if you don't believe me, ask that fascist security guard from last night. She came flying out of the zoo yesterday with her long braid and her attitude, saying I wasn't allowed to protest that lame party."

"Wait a minute, that doesn't seem right," Zach said. "Sophia said you're always out here protesting, and that's not against the law."

"Well, that's what I said," Jersey retorted. "I had almost finished spray-painting the zoo's wall when she made some whole scene about vandalism being illegal."

"Oh," Zach said. "Yeah, vandalizing stuff is totally against the law."

Jersey rolled her eyes dramatically. "Ugh! That's what the cops said when they rolled up. They took away my spray paint and everything, and then they made me leave the zoo. So stupid."

Vishal eyed the stone walls that flanked the zoo's entrance gates. "I don't see any spray paint now."

Jersey pointed to the patch of fresh gray paint on one of the walls. "They painted over it already."

"Well, isn't that convenient," Sophia said, her voice dripping with sarcasm.

"Whatever," Jersey said. "I don't have to prove

anything to you. I know I didn't do anything wrong."

"You mean other than vandalizing public property?" Sophia shot back.

"Listen, I hate to break it to you, but I'm not really worried about what a couple of bratty kids think of me, okay? I have better things to do." Jersey turned away from them and shoved a leaflet at a young couple with a toddler. The man frowned and took the flyer before throwing it away in the nearest trash can without even looking at it.

It was obvious that Jersey had nothing more to say to them, so the four friends walked back into the zoo. "Do you think she's telling the truth?" Zach asked. He walked over to the flamingo exhibit and put a quarter in a nearby machine. He turned the crank and a handful of small dry pellets landed in his palm. He sniffed at them. "Man, I don't know what flamingos eat, but whatever it is, it stinks."

"I'm pretty sure it's shrimp or something. Isn't that why they're pink?" Evie plucked a few bits of food from his hand and tossed them into the exhibit's pond. "I believe Jersey," she said thoughtfully. "She obviously cares a lot about animals. I don't think she would lie about something as serious as a missing red panda." The flamingos flapped at one another and fished out the floating pellets, swishing their beaks back and forth in the water.

Sophia put another quarter in the machine and turned the crank with short, angry jerks. "Ugh, you guys are so naive." The food spilled out of the machine, half of it scattering onto the pavement and missing Sophia's hand completely. She ignored it. "The woman is obviously a criminal. She already admitted to vandalizing the zoo. What more do you want?"

Vishal bent down and swept the fallen pellets into his hand. "Chill, Sophia. Just because someone is guilty of one thing doesn't mean they're guilty of *everything*." He tossed the pieces one by one into the far side of the pond, where a smaller flamingo with mottled pink-and-gray feathers stood by itself. It eagerly guzzled up the unexpected bounty. "Besides, we can easily find out if Jersey's telling the truth." He stepped over to a passing security officer. "Excuse me, Officer Eylon?" he said, reading the guard's name tag. "There was a security guard working at the party here last night. She had long, dark hair in a braid down her back. Do you know if she's working today?"

The officer stroked his neatly trimmed red beard. "Oh, you must be talking about Kristin Tongson. She's on duty in the security office today." He pointed out a spot on the zoo map, and the kids thanked him before making their way to a brown brick building behind the photo booths.

The security office was part of the staff building, and the kids passed a meeting room and a sad-looking break room before they found Officer Tongson sitting behind a long counter in the security office. She was bent over a clipboard of paperwork, her long, dark eyelashes fluttering as she read. A small bank of TV monitors mounted to the walls behind her showed several angles of the zoo entrance, the main gift shop, and a loading bay.

"Hi," Vishal said, flashing a confident grin.

Officer Tongson looked up. "Well, hello again. What can I do for you?"

"My friend here thinks she might have dropped

her phone at the donor party last night when we were getting on the tram." He pointed at Sophia, who tried her best to look like a person who had recently lost a phone. "We were wondering if you might have found it last night."

"Oh, that's too bad," the guard said. "I don't know what I would do without my phone. You must be so upset!"

Sophia clutched her hands together over her heart like a damsel in distress and let out a lofty sigh. "Oh, I'm just devastated!" She blinked her eyes and gazed mournfully up at the ceiling. "I don't know what on earth I'll do if I don't find it!"

Vishal nudged her with his elbow. "Take it down a notch," he said under his breath.

Sophia dropped her hands. "Yeah, no. I mean, I just really need it," she said quickly.

Officer Tongson gave Sophia a strange look and nodded slowly. "Okay," she said. "I don't remember finding anything last night, but let's take a look in the lost and found." She pulled a clear plastic bin from a shelf and plopped it on the counter. After a few moments of rummaging, she gave a regretful shrug. "Sorry, hon. It looks like mostly jackets and pacifiers, and an occasional one of these." She held up a tiny baby shoe and sighed. "Poor parents, right? I don't think these things ever stay on."

"Are you sure nobody found anything?" Vishal pressed. "Maybe you could check the security tapes and see where she might have dropped it?" The officer looked uncertain, and Vishal nudged Sophia again.

"Oh, please, Officer Tongson! It would mean so much if we could at least check!" In a flash of inspiration she added, "My parents will absolutely *kill* me if they know I lost my phone again!"

The officer's face softened, and she gave a conspiratorial grin. "Strict parents, huh? Mine were the worst. I was always getting in trouble for losing stuff!" She clicked a few buttons on the keyboard. "Let's see what we can find."

"Thank you so much, Officer Tongson," Sophia gushed.

"You can call me Kris." The monitor switched to the first guests arriving at the zoo for the previous night's dinner. The walls of the zoo entrance were clearly visible, and the kids could see Jersey waving her sign in the background as various familiar faces greeted the staff and boarded the trams inside. Kris sped up the tape, skimming quickly through the images.

Evie saw herself and her friends appear onscreen, and she knew that if Kris noticed, she would stop the tape before they could see Jersey. She tapped the counter near Kris's hand and pointed to the guard's elaborate gel manicure. "OMG, I *love* your nails! May I see?"

"Oh, thanks!" Kris held out her hands, and Evie oohed and ahhed over the pink-and-gold pattern tipped with tiny crystals. Evie glanced at the TV screen. The last of the guests had driven off in the cart, and Jersey was just walking toward the entrance.

Kris's eyes moved toward the monitor, and Evie pulled out her phone. "Can I take a picture?"

"Sure! Just do a close-up, though. I only started working here a few days ago, so I don't want my new boss to see it and think I'm slacking off on the job." She carefully arranged her hands on the counter, and Evie snapped a few photos.

Kris glanced up to the monitors and saw the police escorting Jersey across the parking lot back to her car. "Oh, my gosh! You should not be seeing that," she said quickly, and turned off the film.

"Oh, no worries," Vishal said easily. "We won't say anything."

Kris looked relieved. "Thanks." She put the lost and found bin back on the shelf. "And I'm sorry about your phone," she said to Sophia. "Did you guys see anything that might help you figure out where it might be?"

Zach nodded. "I think we got what we needed."

The teens thanked the security guard for her help, and Zach pulled the others into the empty break room. It had a sagging, torn couch and a scarred lunch table with a few plastic chairs scattered around it. A TV showed the local news with the sound turned off. "The time stamps on the security video show that Jersey never went inside the zoo last night. And the cops escorted her out by eight forty, which was about half an hour before Nikki discovered that Marvin was missing."

"Yeah, but she could have snuck back in after they all left," Sophia said.

"I don't know," Vishal said. "That would be cutting it pretty tight. She'd have to circle back, hide her car somewhere, sneak into the zoo, get to Marvin's exhibit, and use the meat to lure him into a carrier. Then she would have to sneak him out again, all without being seen by anyone. That's a lot to do in half an hour."

"Vishal's right," Evie said to Sophia. "I know you don't like Jersey, but the timeline just makes it way too hard for her to be the likely culprit."

"But not impossible," Sophia countered. "So I'm keeping her on the list of suspects."

Evie sighed. "Fine. Whatever." She folded her arms. "You always do what you want anyway."

"You guys." Zach grabbed Evie's shoulder and pointed at the TV. "What's happening?" City Councilman Tommy Brown stood behind a podium in front of a makeshift crowd near the zoo's front gates. His once-affable face was hardened into a stern glower, bushy white eyebrows pushed low above his eyes. His leathery pink forehead was shiny with perspiration, and he pointed vigorously at the zoo entrance. An inset photo of Marvin flashed up on the corner of the screen, and it was quickly joined by an image of B-17.

Vishal grabbed the remote and turned up the volume. "How long must we continue to tolerate this menace in our midst?" the councilman demanded. "This brazen animal broke into the zoo and killed Marvin, a beloved city icon, right under our noses. If we don't stop it now, what's next? Our pets? Our *children*?" The crowd murmured angrily in front of him.

"What is this?" Evie asked. "What's he saying?"

"I want to pledge to all of you standing here today, that as your city councilman—and, God willing, some-day soon as your city's mayor"—at this, a huge cheer erupted from the crowd, and Brown allowed himself a small smile—"I will do everything in my power to keep our zoo animals, our pets, and, most of all, our children safe from dangerous wildlife like B-17. And so it is with great pride that I stand here today to tell you that I have introduced a city ordinance banning wild predators from our borders, and I have called upon our leaders to vote next Monday to have B-17 destroyed once and for all. This is *our* city, and I won't allow its citizens to live in terror anymore!" The crowd erupted in cheers, and the gaggle of reporters near the podium pushed forward, shouting questions. Brown simply waved them off with a grandfatherly smile and turned to shake hands with a cluster of gray-suited business-men, who grinned and slapped his back, pumping his arm up and down vigorously.

The news switched to weather, and Vishal clicked off the television. There was a long silence as the kids stared at the empty screen, stunned at what they had just witnessed. Finally, Vishal spoke. "Did he just say he wants the city to *kill* B-17?"

Sophia's voice was bitter. "Yup."

"But she's innocent!" Vishal protested.

"Of course she is, but even if they knew that, it probably wouldn't make any difference," Sophia said. "This is what always happens with wildlife. We poison their water, take their food supply, and destroy their habitat, and when they manage to find a way to survive anyway, we kill them, too. When people pick a fight with animals, the animals always lose."

"But maybe if we bring our suspicions to the city council, we can clear B-17's name and keep her from being killed for something she didn't do," Evie said. "After all, what happened to 'innocent until proven guilty'?"

Zach raised an eyebrow at his sister. "Do you really need to ask?" He sighed. "Suspicions aren't enough. The city isn't going to listen to us unless we can prove who *really* took Marvin," Zach said.

Vishal stood up. "Let's see if we can check the security tape again," he suggested. "Maybe we missed something: someone climbing over a wall or carrying a suspicious package. There has to be some kind of clue we can use."

When the kids returned to the security office, Kris was leaning over the back desk, peering intently at a computer monitor and tapping some buttons on the keyboard. "Excuse me, Kris?" Sophia began politely.

Kris whirled around, startled. Before she could say anything, Zach held up his hand. "Stop right there!" he cried. "If you touch that keyboard again, we're calling the cops!"

# CHAPTER
# 10

Kris froze.

"What's on that security video?" Zach demanded.

"Nothing!" Kris said quickly.

"Oh, come on," Zach said. "Anyone can see that's you in that video. What were you doing sneaking around in the bushes outside the zoo when you were supposed to be working at the party?"

Kris rose up to her full height and looked imperiously down her nose. She cleared her throat, and when she spoke, her voice was low and official-sounding. "I received a report of something suspicious in the bushes, so obviously I was investigating it. That's the only thing this video shows."

Zach folded his arms. "Oh, really? Then

why are you trying to erase it?"

Kris's eyes shifted, and she folded her arms defensively across her chest. "I wasn't."

"Then I guess you won't mind if we show this to your supervisor," Vishal said, walking toward the computer.

"No!" Kris shouted, jumping in front of him.

Vishal stopped, and all four kids stared her down until she finally broke. "Okay, fine. I wasn't investigating a strange sound." She sank down into a nearby chair, and her voice dropped. "I was looking for my keys," she mumbled.

"What?" Evie asked.

Kris dropped her head. "My set of security keys. When I got back to my post at the party I noticed they weren't on my belt, and I thought they might have come off in the altercation with Ms. Sinclair. I've only been on the job for a few days, and if my boss knew my keys had gone missing, I would be fired for sure."

"Did you find them?" Vishal asked.

"Not right away," Kris admitted. "They weren't at the entrance. But I found them when I got back to the party."

Sophia's eyes sharpened. "Where were they?"

"It was a warm night, so I had taken off my jacket and dropped it on the seat of one of the extra carts. I found my keys in the pocket." She put her head in her hands. "My boss would kill me if he found out I was that careless." She lifted her head again and looked earnestly at the teens. "The funny thing is, I could have sworn I had them clipped to my belt. That's where I always put them. I still can't believe I would have done something so dumb as to leave them in my jacket like that."

Evie and Zach looked at each other. "Do you remember the last time you had your keys?"

Kris picked up a pen and doodled on the yellow message pad near the phone, thinking. Finally, she said, "I know I had them right before I got the vandalism call, because I used them to unlock the bathroom for some guests." Her pen drew a swirl pattern on the yellow paper. "That was probably eight ten or so."

"And when did you find them again?" Evie asked.

"Just before nine o'clock." The guard put down the pen. "Listen, you aren't going to tell my boss or anything about this, are you?" Her voice was pleading. "I love animals, and I really need this job. Besides, nobody even knew the keys were missing. I promise I'll be more careful next time."

"Are you kidding?" Sophia asked. "You lost a set of keys that unlocks every enclosure and building in the entire zoo! Give me one good reason why I shouldn't have you fired."

"OMG, Sophia, she said she was sorry. Chill out!" Evie turned to the security guard. "Don't worry; your secret's safe with us."

"Wait," Sophia said. "No it isn't! I'm telling—" Before she could say any more, Evie and the boys had dragged her by the elbow out of the room and down the hall.

When they arrived outside, Sophia shook them off. "What was that about?!" she asked angrily.

"We could ask you the same thing," Evie said sternly. "You don't go around threatening to have people fired."

"Why not?" Sophia challenged.

"Well, for one thing, it makes you sound like an obnoxious, spoiled brat," Evie said.

Sophia bristled. "No, it doesn't."

Vishal smiled good-naturedly. "Oh, it *totally* does." He ran his hand through his hair. "Like you know how in the movies there's the hero, and then there's some entitled character that everyone loves to hate? Free advice: The heroes are never the ones running around threatening to have people fired."

Sophia waved her hand. "Well, maybe they should be. That guard's carelessness put the entire zoo in danger. It was probably her keys that Marvin's kidnapper used to break into his enclosure, you know."

"Of course we know," Zach said, "but did you hear her? She swore she remembered clipping them to her belt. Maybe the kidnapper took them off her belt and snuck them back in her jacket pocket later."

"But that means Marvin's kidnapper would have to be someone at the donor dinner," Evie said.

"Exactly," Vishal agreed. "Does anyone remember who all was there last night?"

"Mostly," Sophia said, "but I can't remember everyone."

Zach brightened. "Our gift bags! I'm pretty sure we

had souvenir photos in them, didn't we?"

"Mine was just of the four of us with Shakti, though," Evie said. "Anyone have something different?"

"Mine is a big group photo from the dinner," Vishal said. "I put it on my bulletin board when I got home last night. Let's meet at my house after school tomorrow and use it to make a list of suspects."

\*\*\*

It was a quiet bus ride to Vishal's house the next day. Each teen was still deep in thought about which of the zoo's donors would want to take Marvin and why. Zach rested his head against the bus window. He ran the list of guests through his mind, trying to remember if any of them had acted suspiciously or disappeared for long stretches of time. He had been so excited about seeing all of the animals that the rest of the night's details were a little fuzzy.

When they arrived at the Desai family's duplex, Vishal unlocked the front door and kicked off his sneakers, tossing them in the vague direction of a crammed shoe rack near the door. Sophia watched Evie and Zach do the same, Zach neatly arranging the twins' shoes before joining his sister on the bright-orange sofa. Sophia paused in the doorway. Finally she bent down and slowly removed her suede sneakers, placing them gently on the floor next to Zach's. The faded silk rug felt soft beneath her feet, and she admired its magenta ikat pattern, bright against the dark-wood floor. Vibrant canvases covered the ochre walls, their bold, abstract designs filling the room with light and warmth. "I love your house," Sophia said. "The artwork is so cool."

Vishal shrugged. "They're my mom's. She's a painter."

"Is she home?" Zach asked.

"She's probably working," Vishal answered. "Let me check." He stepped into the kitchen and glanced at the arrangement of wooden magnets on the fridge. One large magnet at the top said MOM IS . . . and an assortment of smaller magnets was clustered beneath, with phrases like RUNNING ERRANDS, NAPPING, and TAKING A WALK. The magnet marked WORKING was pushed to the top. Vishal ducked his head back into the living room. "Yup. She's at her studio. Why don't you guys grab a snack while I get the photo?"

Sophia watched dumbstruck as Zach and Evie hopped off the couch and descended on the kitchen like professionals, finishing each other's sentences as they opened cabinet doors and rummaged through the fridge. "Do they still have—" Evie asked, pulling out a clear plastic container of papadum from the cabinet.

"Chutneys? Right here. Green and tamarind," Zach answered. "There's also some hummus. Maybe we could have that with—"

"Red pepper? Is there a fresh one we can cut up?" Evie asked.

Zach tossed the pepper to his sister, who had already pulled out a cutting board and knife. Evie rinsed the pepper in the sink and laid it flat on the wooden surface.

"You two are really twinning out in here. How do you know where everything is?" Sophia asked.

"Vishal's our best friend," Evie said. She expertly sliced the pepper, tossing the core and seeds into the compost bin under the sink. "We've known one another since we were babies. Don't you do the same with your best friends?" She arranged the pepper slices on the plate with the hummus and handed it to Sophia.

Sophia blushed. "I guess not." She put the plate on the kitchen island and looked timidly at the floor. "I kinda thought that, you know, *you guys* were my best friends."

Zach and Evie looked at each other in surprise. They liked hanging out with Sophia, but they hadn't really considered her a best friend, at least not like Vishal. Vishal's friendship was solid; his life was thoroughly woven in with theirs, like three trees whose roots had grown together. Sophia flitted in and out of their lives like a butterfly. They texted with her a lot, and they sometimes saw her on weekends, but she usually seemed to be busy with ballet classes, Mandarin lessons, or some charity project or another. She was a good friend, but they had always imagined she had closer friends from outside of school that she spent time with.

Vishal appeared in the doorway, souvenir photo in hand. His spiky hair was mussed, and a dust bunny hung from his sleeve. "Sorry. It fell behind my bed."

His forehead wrinkled. "Ooh. Weird energy in here. What's up?"

"Nothing!" Sophia said quickly. She cleared her throat and tucked her hair behind her ear. "I think the snack's almost ready."

"Sweet!" Vishal's lanky arm made a beeline for the papadum, but Evie blocked him.

"Eww! Wash your hands first! You look like you've been rolling around the inside of a vacuum cleaner."

Vishal ineffectively brushed at the lint that covered his dark hoodie and swiped his hands across his pant legs. "There! Good as new!" Evie wordlessly pointed at the sink, and Vishal sighed, slouched over, and began to wash his hands.

"With soap," Evie commanded. Another loud sigh came from the vicinity of the sink, and the water turned back on again.

Vishal returned to the kitchen island, his hands leaving a trail of dripping water in his wake.

"Dude, seriously?" Zach asked. "Now even *I'm* offended." He tossed a dish towel to Vishal. "You're gonna get the papadums all soggy." He pulled a pen and paper out of the kitchen junk drawer. "Okay. Time to make our list of suspects. We just have to research every person from the party and figure out who would have a motive to steal Marvin."

"Don't forget opportunity," Evie said. "Every table was full during dinner, so Marvin could only have been taken either before dinner or afterward, when everyone broke into groups to see Shakti."

"We didn't get up to the elephant pavilion until about six fifty or so, and dinner was at seven fifteen. That leaves a pretty short window, but it's possible," Sophia said.

Vishal shook his head. "It couldn't have happened then. Remember, Nikki checked on Marvin just after seven thirty, and he was still in his enclosure. He had to have been kidnapped after dinner, sometime between eight and nine fifteen."

The group bent over the souvenir photo from the donor dinner. It was already wrinkled and a little wilted from the short time it had been in Vishal's possession. Smiling guests crowded around Councilman Brown as he held up his Golden Gorilla Award.

Zach studied the faces carefully. Did anyone look preoccupied or nervous, like someone who was about to commit a crime? He clicked the pen and started writing down names. "Okay. There's that old couple. I remember his striped sweatband and her big purse."

"The Forshentskys," Sophia added. "They come to every event. I'm always worried that Lloyd is going to fall down and break his hip; he's so frail, he looks like he's made of dead leaves or something. But Jackie says they still love getting out and coming to the zoo." She pointed to the round-faced city councilman holding up his Golden Gorilla Award. "And there's Big Tommy Brown, with Dr. Chang standing next to him." Dr. Chang had his hand on the councilman's shoulder like they were old friends.

Evie tapped another face in the photo. "And we have Gideon and his game show host smile giving the thumbs-up right here. There's Abby next to him with that huge engagement ring on her finger. She always looks like she'd rather be at home with her dogs or out hiking somewhere, doesn't she?"

Vishal pointed at the curly-haired, olive-skinned man wearing shiny loafers with no socks. "And there's Dante Fishman, the Monkeyfart guy. What's his girlfriend's name? The one with the fox-fur coat?"

Sophia rolled her eyes. "Bitsy. I still can't believe she would wear fur to an animal event! It's beyond tacky. I mean, the zoo actually has a fox exhibit! I hate fur. It's just cruel and unnecessary."

"Huh," Evie said.

"What?" Sophia asked.

"It just sounds like something Jersey would say."

"Well, Jersey's not the only one who cares about animals." Suddenly Sophia's eyes widened. "Wait a minute. Jersey said that she *and her group* were planning an action at the donor dinner. What if the spray-painting was only a distraction? What if the real action was taking Marvin?"

"Yeah, but then we're back to the keys again," Vishal said. "No outside person could have gotten Kris's keys."

Sophia's eyes sparkled. "I'm not saying it was an outside person. I think someone in this photo is secretly a member of SCAT!"

TONIGHT'S DINNER
HONORING LONGTIME
___ OF THE ZOO

COUNCILMAN
TOM BROWN

# CHAPTER
# 11

A short time later, the four friends snacked silently, each hunched over a laptop as they researched the guests.

"I don't even know why I'm bothering with the Forshentskys," Sophia said. "They obviously didn't do it. After all, they've been major donors to the zoo for years, and SCAT hates zoos. Besides, Lloyd's arms would probably break off if he tried to lift up a red panda. He can barely even hold Jackie's purse for her!"

"I don't even think *I* could hold Jackie's purse," Zach said. "That thing is massive!"

"Massive enough to hold a red panda?" Evie asked.

"Doubtful," Sophia answered. "Even if it could, Marvin would be scratching at it, trying to get out. It would be pretty obvious. He must have been hidden in a carrier crate somewhere and retrieved later. There are a million good hiding spots in the zoo, especially for carrier crates. The zoo uses them all the time to transport animals, so you could practically hide it in plain sight."

"Okay, so the Forshentskys are out," Evie said. "What about Dante or his girlfriend?"

"The one in the fur coat?" Sophia asked. "I don't think so. Jersey's such a hardcore vegan, she wouldn't feed meat to a starving tiger. There's no way anyone from SCAT would wear fur."

"Sure, fine, but what about Dante? He could have done it," Evie said. "What have you found out about him so far, Vish?"

"It says here that he went to Dartmouth." Vishal clicked through Dante's various social media pages. "Let's see if it lists what clubs he was in." He tapped the mouse a few times. "He was in an a capella group called the Sharp Fellas. Unexpected. Annnnd . . . here's some photos of him on a deer-hunting trip for his friend's bachelor party." Vishal turned the screen to show a grinning Dante and his friends proudly crouched around a dead stag.

Sophia curled her lip in disgust. "Ugh. No thanks."

"You eat meat, Sophia," Evie said. "What's wrong with hunting?"

"I'm not saying something's wrong with it," Sophia said. "I just don't want to do it."

"Me neither," Zach said. "I prefer imagining that my meat comes straight from the supermarket."

"Not me," Evie said. "I'd rather eat a normal animal that had a normal life than some poor creature crammed into a tiny cage where it couldn't even turn around."

"We only eat organic, grass-fed, and cage-free, so I don't have to worry about that," Sophia said.

"Must be nice," Evie muttered. "That stuff is expensive."

Zach scratched Dante's name off the list. "We've already eliminated four people; we're running out of suspects." He looked at the scattering of remaining names. "I mean, the zoo director's hardly going to be a member of SCAT, so he's out." He pushed the list away in frustration. "I can't find ties between any of these people and animal rights groups." He leaned back and folded his arms. "I don't know. Maybe we should start looking for another motive."

Sophia leaned over her laptop. "Or maybe we're searching in the wrong place." She turned the monitor around to show SCAT's website. "I was poking around Jersey's website. It's a pretty rinky-dink setup, but I thought it might have old lists of members or something like that. No such luck, but I did find photos from past events. And guess who I found!"

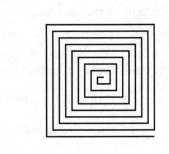

# CHAPTER
## 12

"That's Abigail Morris," Evie said with surprise. "*She's* a member of SCAT?"

"That gives her motive *and* opportunity," Sophia said. "While Jersey was providing a distraction at the front of the zoo, Abby must have stolen Kris's keys, hidden Marvin in a carrier somewhere, and left a fake bobcat print to throw us off the scent." She folded her arms smugly. "I never trusted her."

"Oh, get over yourself, Sophia. You totally trusted her," Evie retorted. "We all did." Her face clouded in doubt. "In fact, I still have a hard time believing she would do this, especially if it meant implicating B-17. Abby seemed so excited when we showed her that photo."

"*Seemed* being the key word," Sophia shot back. "She's obviously a huge liar, so why should we believe anything she says or does?"

"But framing B-17 for the crime put a target on the bobcat's back. The city wants to kill her!" Zach said.

"Abby couldn't have known that would happen. In fact, she's probably consumed with guilt over it, knowing that her rash actions have put B-17 in jeopardy." Sophia rubbed her hands together. "I bet if we use that against her, we can crack her like an egg."

The others just stared at her. "Get her to confess," Sophia explained. "Geez, don't you guys ever watch detective shows?"

\*\*\*

Abby's face broke into a broad smile when she opened her door to find the four young detectives on her front porch. Her pit bull mix, Ronin, squeezed past her to take a victory lap of joy around the yard before shoving her favorite toy in Vishal's hand. He tossed it, and the black-and-white dog galloped across the yard to retrieve it. Thumbelina Feathertail pranced at their feet on her three legs, fluffy tail fluttering in the air like a banner.

Zach bent down to pet the little dog. "Come on in," Abby said.

"Where's Chicken?" Evie asked, looking for the tiny, toothless old Maltese.

"She's napping," Abby explained. "Now that she's lost her hearing completely, it takes a lot to wake her up these days."

The group settled in on the sofas of Abby's cozy little living room. She shared the house with her parents, and three people's accumulated collection of books filled every available shelf. There was even a tall pile next to the easy chair by the window.

"I heard about Marvin," Abby said. "Are you four doing okay?"

"No," Sophia said bluntly. She folded her arms and narrowed her eyes. "I suppose you also heard about B-17?"

Abby's face hardened. "I did, and I'm furious. What kind of backward city council would advocate for the destruction of a beautiful, innocent animal?"

Sophia pounced like a cat. "So you know that B-17 is innocent?"

"Of course she's innocent. All animals are! Eating Marvin was just in her nature; we can't blame her for that. As soon as I heard the news, I called MEOWS to see if there's anything I can do to help." Thumbelina hopped onto Abby's lap, and Abby stroked her idly. "And believe me, I made it very clear to Gideon that we will not be supporting that blowhard Tommy Brown's run for mayor anymore."

"I must say, that's a pretty robust response," Sophia said. "Methinks the lady doth protest too much, don't you?" She turned to her friends for support, but they just gaped at her.

"What is she talking about?" Vishal whispered.

"Dude, I have no idea," Zach whispered back. "She lost me at 'robust.'" Vishal tittered.

"For Pete's sake, you guys, it's a Shakespeare reference! Hasn't anyone seen *Hamlet* around here? Seriously, keep up!" She pointed at Abby. "I'm trying to say that she's going out of her way to act all innocent, which just goes to prove that she's guilty."

"Guilty of what?" Abby asked.

"See?" Sophia crowed. "That's exactly what a guilty

person would say!"

"Or an innocent person who has no idea what you're talking about," Zach pointed out.

"Or a guilty person who has done so many terrible deeds, they aren't sure which one the speaker is referencing," Vishal added. Evie kicked him in the foot. "What? I'm just saying."

"Can we all please stay on track?" Sophia yanked her laptop out of her bag. "I'm trying to accuse someone of something, and you're ruining my momentum!"

"What exactly am I being accused of?" Abby asked with amusement.

"This!" Sophia opened her laptop with a flourish and pointed to the SCAT photo. "*You* are a member of SCAT! You hate zoos and everything they stand for, so there's only one reason you'd come to a donor event at the zoo: to kidnap Marvin!"

Abby blushed a deep red, and Sophia cackled in triumphant glee.

"Is it true?" Evie asked. "Did you kidnap Marvin for SCAT?"

There was a long pause. "No," Abby said finally. "It's

true I was a member of SCAT at one time. I've always loved animals, and SCAT's mission was dedicated to protecting the rights of captive animals. We protested cruelty in greyhound racing and factory farming, and we even worked with other organizations to lobby for stricter penalties for animal abusers."

Evie looked sideways at Sophia. "Wow. That sounds a lot like stuff I've heard you talk about," she said pointedly. Sophia refused to look at her.

"But there were other things about SCAT that I didn't agree with," Abby continued, "Jersey and I used to stay up all night debating things like pets or zoos or eating meat. At first it was fun; we didn't agree on everything, but we still listened to each other. She was a really good friend." Abby hugged her dog closer. "Then over time, things changed. Jersey's views got more extreme, and sometimes in SCAT meetings she would treat me more like an enemy than a friend. I thought we all still had the same goal, but somehow that didn't seem to matter anymore. A bunch of the original members ended up leaving, and the newer folks were more like Jersey. When I finally left the group,

Jersey called me a traitor and told me not to bother coming back." She gave a sad shrug. "We haven't spoken since."

Evie looked over at Sophia, who was silent. Finally, Zach spoke. "So you *don't* think zoos are evil, and that's why you quit the group?"

Abby nodded. "I've always liked zoos, actually. And I think they do a lot to make people want to help animals that they would normally never have the chance to see. It's much easier to care about elephants if you've seen one in real life." She leaned back in the sofa. "It's still a secret, but I may as well tell you that the reason we were at the dinner is because Gideon's wedding gift to me is a big donation to the zoo. We're helping to build a new orangutan exhibit."

"Wow!" Vishal said. "That's so cool!"

Abby smiled. "I'm pretty excited, actually."

Evie nudged Sophia with her elbow. "Isn't that great, Sophia?"

Sophia's normally perfect posture was slumped in defeat. So far all of her leads had taken them straight to nowhere. "Yeah, I guess," she said listlessly.

"What's wrong?" Zach asked her. "You look miserable." Before she could answer, Zach turned to Abby. "Wait a minute. You just talked about how excited you are about helping the zoo, but *you* looked miserable in all the photos from the donor dinner. How come?"

Abby let out a long sigh. "I was mad at Gideon. First he made that mean crack about Jersey on the tram, and then the minute we arrived at the cocktail hour, he got into an argument with Darwin." She twisted her engagement ring around her finger. "He's so charming and sweet with me. I don't know why he can't just be that way with everyone."

"Yeah," Evie said, thinking of Sophia. Maybe there was some kind of rich people disease that made them nice to their friends but rude to everyone else. "Did he say what the argument was about?" She wondered if Gideon could be the mystery person they had heard quarreling with Dr. Chang before dinner. She snuck a glance at Sophia to see if she was thinking the same thing, but Sophia was looking down at her hands.

Abby shook her head. "He wouldn't tell me. He just said it was stupid and he didn't want to talk about it."

Ronin got up from her dog bed and shoved a toy in Abby's hand. She tossed it, and the dog caught it in the air before bringing it back. "I thought he had shaken it off, but then when it was time for us to meet Shakti, I couldn't find him anywhere. I checked my phone, and I found this text."

# CHAPTER
# 13

The young detectives looked in shock at Gideon's text message. Had he just confessed to stealing Marvin to get back at Dr. Chang? "Was he still waiting out front of the zoo when you left?" Vishal asked.

"He pulled up a minute or two after I got off the tram at the entrance," Abby answered. "He said he had taken a drive to cool his head."

*Or to drop off a stolen panda somewhere,* Vishal thought. He tried to keep his expression neutral, but he saw Abby read the doubt in his face.

"Listen, I know Gideon. He may be a bull in a china shop sometimes, but he's all talk. He would never do something like that. Besides, he and I agreed that there would be no more secrets between us."

"But if that's true, then why wouldn't he tell you what the argument with Dr. Chang was about?" Zach asked gently.

Abby paled. "I don't know," she finally said.

*\*\**

The next day after school, Vishal and the twins stood at the flagpole waiting for Sophia. "Where is she?" Vishal asked. "She knows we're going to go interview Gideon. You'd think she'd be the first one out here."

"She wasn't at lunch. Maybe she went home sick or something," Zach said. "She was really quiet the whole way home from Abby's house yesterday. Not even Edgar could get her to crack a smile."

"She would have told us if she wasn't coming." Evie pulled out her phone. "I'll text her." But just as she was about to start typing, she noticed Sophia slipping out a side door and walking in the opposite direction toward the parking lot. "Sophia!" Evie waved her arms over her head. "We're over here!" Sophia put her head down and picked up her pace. Evie looked at the boys. "Do you think she didn't hear me?"

"Doubtful," Zach said. "I'm pretty sure people in

space can hear you when you yell." Evie playfully shoved her brother.

"Let's catch up with her," Vishal suggested. He broke into a trot and the twins followed. They arrived at the parking lot just in time to see the shiny black SUV pulling away with Sophia inside.

"That was weird," Zach said. "Do you think she forgot?"

"No way she would forget," Vishal replied. "Sophia lives for this stuff!"

"Maybe she had a last-minute doctor's appointment or something," Evie said, but she didn't really believe it. Vishal was right. Sophia loved being part of the Gemini Detective Agency. She would have to be tied to a chair to miss a chance to interrogate a suspect. Something was wrong. Evie reached for her phone again.

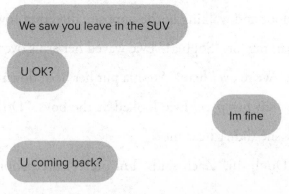

We saw you leave in the SUV

U OK?

Im fine

U coming back?

Questioning Gideon today

Sorry I forgot

I have a Mandarin lesson

Just go without me

Evie stared down at the text. "Has Sophia been kidnapped by aliens? She'd rather go to her Mandarin lesson? Since when?"

"Maybe that wasn't really Sophia," Vishal said. "Maybe it was a clone. Or a robot. They can make very realistic robots these days."

"Come on, I'm serious. This isn't like her. Something's up."

"Look, she says she's fine." Vishal checked his watch. "If we want to get the next downtown bus, we've gotta go. I want to find out what that argument was about between Gideon and Dr. Chang, don't you? We can fill Sophia in later."

Zach saw Evie hesitate. "It'll be okay, Evie. Maybe Sophia just needs some space or something. Right now we just have to let her be."

Evie followed the boys on the bus, but the whole ride over, she felt a tiny knot forming in her stomach. Sophia might not be her closest friend, but she was an important part of the Gemini Detective Agency. It felt strange to follow a lead without her. But Zach was right. They couldn't put the case on hold because of Sophia. Saving B-17 was too important.

Gideon's new offices were in a historic downtown building with a black marble lobby and elevator doors that were covered with elaborate gold grillwork. After finding Gideon's office number on the directory, the three stepped into the oak-paneled elevator and pushed the button for the eighth floor. "So, do we have a plan?" Zach asked. "Because we really need a plan. Let's make a list of questions to ask so we don't forget anything."

Vishal stretched, exposing a thin strip of belly under his T-shirt and hoodie. "No, dude. I say we just wing it. Take him by surprise. We don't want to give anything away."

"I'm not saying *we tell* Gideon our plan," Zach said. "We can list our questions beforehand and still take him by surprise. How would Gideon know what we were going to ask?"

"We might give something away subliminally. He'll just sense it, you know? Pick up our vibe."

Zach bristled. "Is Gideon psychic all of a sudden? How is he gonna *pick up our vibe*?"

Vishal shrugged. "I don't know; he just will."

"Seriously? That's not even a real reason!" Zach threw up his hands. "All I ask is if *for once* we could take five minutes to make a plan before we go rushing in, but you guys never listen to me!" He turned to his sister. "Come on, Evie. If you take my side, it'll finally be two against one. What do you say? Plan?"

Evie bumped against her brother. "Sorry, little bro, but this whole not-listening-to-you thing has worked out pretty well so far. I say we keep it going."

"I hate it when you call me 'little bro,'" Zach said. "You're only seven minutes older than me."

Evie patted her brother on the head. "And I'll never let you forget it."

Zach was ready with a sharp retort, but before he could speak, the elevator doors opened and the others strode quickly down the hall. Zach scurried after them, cursing inwardly at the disloyalty of best friends and sisters.

Gideon's new offices were smaller and less flashy than the vast glass-and-chrome space they remembered from their previous run-in. In the reception area, leather chairs flanked a glass-topped brass table that held a perfectly arranged fan of glossy business magazines. The gleaming wood reception desk was empty, and the kids could hear Gideon talking loudly on the phone down the hall. Their feet sank into the thick pile carpet, and when they heard a piercing bray of laughter behind a heavy oak door, they knew they had found the right office.

The door was slightly ajar, so Evie gave it a quick tap. "I'll call you back," she heard him say before he shouted, "Come in!" Gideon was ready with his trademark megawatt smile when Evie pushed open the door, but his face fell when he recognized the young detectives. "Oh, it's you."

Evie smiled nervously. "Yep, it's us." No one said anything. There was a leather sofa and several expensive chairs in the room, but Gideon didn't invite them to sit down. Evie cast an uncertain glance over at Zach, who was looking at her reproachfully. Evie knew from those tightly pressed-together lips and sternly waggling eyebrows that Zach had probably been right about making a plan, and he knew it. *Ugh,* Evie thought. *I hate it when he knows he's right.* Now what?

There was a soft *thunk* as Vishal flopped down on the buttery leather sofa and stretched out his lanky legs, ankles peeping out of pants that were somehow always an inch too short. "Hey, Gideon. What's new?" His confidence seemed to shake Gideon, who blinked in surprise and suddenly seemed very busy with papers on his desk.

*How does Vishal do that?* Evie wondered. *How does he walk through the world like he just belongs everywhere he goes?* Vishal flashed Zach a smirk; he was winging it, and it was working. Gideon was obviously rattled. Evie sat down in one of the luxurious side chairs in front of the desk and spared a moment of pity for her brother. If Vishal came out triumphant today, Zach was never going to hear the end of it.

"I'm actually pretty swamped right now, as you can see, and I would hate to keep you waiting in this boring old office while I finish." He looked up, his smile tight and brittle. "Why don't you kids run along and play?"

Vishal leaned back on the sofa. "It's okay. Take all the time you need. We don't mind waiting."

Zach perched stiffly on the sofa's edge, trying his best to radiate a confident ability to wing it, although he was pretty sure he just looked like he had to use the bathroom. "Yeah, go ahead; we're very patient." He pulled a little notebook and pen out of his backpack and started scribbling something, hoping he looked like a person who had all the time in the world.

Evie leaned back in her chair and folded her arms, staring Gideon down. She gave him her best *don't-start-none-won't-be-none* face. It seemed to work, because he broke down almost immediately. "Okay, look. What do you want? Abby said you came by yesterday about some kind of missing animal. Merlin? Marcus? Something like that. Anyway, I don't know why you'd want to talk to me. The zoo is Abby's thing, not mine."

"You seem a little on edge," Vishal said. "Is

everything all right?"

"Well, I'm a little irritated, quite frankly," Gideon shot back.

"Oh, really?" Evie leaned forward. "And why might that be?"

"It's hard to put my finger on it, but I think it might have something to do with having my workday interrupted by a gaggle of third-rate teen Sherlocks snapping at shadows like a dog chasing its tail."

*Ouch.* Evie sat back, her cheeks hot with embarrassment. This was going to be harder than they thought. Where was Sophia when they needed her? Sophia was totally immune to cutting remarks; they were like a second language to her. Evie looked back at Vishal and Zach. Vishal's composure seemed to be waning, and Zach was hunched over, scribbling something on a pad. They obviously weren't going to be any help.

"Um, yeah," Evie finally said. "I get it. Nobody likes having their day interrupted." She shrugged. "So maybe if you just answer our questions, we can be on our way."

"What questions?" Gideon said peevishly. "You haven't asked anything."

*Oh, right.* Evie's cheeks were on fire now. This whole interview had gone dramatically off the rails. She couldn't even remember what questions they wanted to ask. Why wasn't Sophia here? Why hadn't they made a plan?

Behind her, Zach cleared his throat. "Thank you for bringing that to our attention," he said smoothly. "Question one: What were you and Dr. Chang arguing about at the donor dinner?"

Gideon scoffed. "What are you talking about? We didn't have an argument."

Zach continued as though Gideon hadn't spoken. "The argument took place between approximately"—he looked down at his notebook—"six fifty-five and seven ten p.m., is that correct?"

"I told you, there wasn't any argument!"

Zach smiled. "There were witnesses. And it was corroborated by your fiancée, Abigail Morris."

Vishal had caught the rhythm now. "Wanna try again?"

"Fine," Gideon huffed. "But it wasn't an argument; it was a small disagreement. It was barely worth mentioning, hardly a big deal."

"But a big enough deal that you left early, missing the chance to meet an *amazing* rhino," Zach said.

"Like I said, animals are Abby's thing, not mine."

"But didn't you want, like, live tigers at your wedding?" Vishal asked.

Gideon flushed. "That's different."

"As I was saying," Zach said, elbowing Vishal sharply, "you left early, leaving your fiancée at the party alone, and the reason you gave for leaving was"—he looked down at his notebook again, milking the moment—"that you were upset about the argument. Is that correct?" Zach kept his face composed, but his insides were dancing with excitement. He was enjoying this. Before Gideon could deny it, Zach smiled again. "We have the texts."

Gideon briefly bared his teeth like a cornered dog. "Fine," he said tightly. "Yes, we had an argument, and yes, I was upset about it. But it wasn't about anything important."

"If it wasn't important, then why wouldn't you tell Abby what it was about?" Evie asked sweetly. A confession was so close, she could almost taste it.

"Because she wouldn't understand. Look, it was stupid, okay? We're funding the new orangutan exhibit, and trust me, kiddo, it's not cheap. So I figure I'm helping out the zoo, why not let the zoo help me?"

"Help you what?" Vishal asked.

"Advertise," Gideon said, unable to believe that the kids had not figured this out for themselves. "I mean, orangutans are monkeys, right?"

"They're apes, actually," Evie said, surprising herself. Wow. Sophia really was rubbing off on her.

Gideon ignored her. "So why not use this donation as a chance to advertise our new app?"

Zach blinked. "So you and the zoo director got in a heated argument over whether or not he would name the new orangutan exhibit after Monkeyfarts Mayhem?"

"We wanted to call it Monkeyfarts Manor, class it up a bit. Just think of all the publicity it would give us, not to mention all the attention it would bring to the zoo. We could leverage that. It's a win-win!"

"Yeah, I'm guessing that was a hard no from Dr. Chang." Vishal snickered. "But I'm not gonna lie. That would have been awesome."

Gideon relaxed. "See? That's a kid who gets it." He stretched back in his chair and put his hands behind his head. "That zoo director's lack of vision was gonna lose me the potential to reach a brand-new audience. Of course I was mad!"

"Mad enough to steal a red panda?" Zach asked.

Gideon laughed and turned back to his computer, dismissing them. "Sorry to burst your bubble, kid, but I wouldn't know a red panda if one came up and smacked me in the face!"

Evie folded her arms. "Oh, cut the crap, Gideon. That's obviously a lie."

# CHAPTER
## 14

Evie pointed to Gideon's monitor. "Your desktop pattern is literally a red panda." Vishal and Zach stood up to see.

"What? No, you must be mistaken." A flustered Gideon quickly pulled up his web browser to hide the panda on the screen. "I don't know what you're talking about." He clicked frantically around, trying to open a new window on the screen.

Vishal pointed to the pull-down menu of book-marked sites. "And RedPandaFanda is one of your favorited sites, dude."

"Fine, okay? Fine!" Gideon snapped. "Yes, I just so happen to love red pandas, but who wouldn't?" He pulled up the RedPandaFanda site, which was littered with adorable photos. "Look at them! Look how cute they are with their little noses!"

"Right?!" Vishal cried. "You just want to boop those little noses, don't you?"

"Yes," Gideon squealed. "I *absolutely* want to boop those little noses." He suddenly remembered himself, and his tone turned serious again. "But that has nothing to do with why I left the donor dinner early. Being a red panda superfan isn't a crime, you know."

"But stealing one is, and it sounds like Dr. Chang knew it. I heard him tell you that what you wanted was illegal and out of the question," Evie said. "I don't think your argument had anything to do with naming the orangutan exhibit."

Gideon sighed. "Whatever, fine, so I lied about the argument. But that was because I knew that if you found out what it was really about, I'd just sound guilty. And I'm not! I had nothing to do with Marvin's disappearance!"

"The argument was about Marvin, though, wasn't it?" Zach asked.

Gideon nodded. "It was stupid and embarrassing."

He looked down at his perfectly manicured nails. "I wasn't lying when I said that the zoo is more Abby's thing than mine. I'd never really given the zoo much thought until she took me there back when we first started dating. And so when Dr. Chang offered us an Adopt an Animal package along with the other perks of our donation, I jumped at the chance to adopt Marvin."

"Oh, no," Evie said. "You didn't."

Gideon continued. "I mean, who could possibly know that when you 'adopt' an animal at the zoo, you don't *really* adopt it?"

"Literally everyone," Evie said.

"I asked Dr. Chang when I could take Marvin home with me, and he looked at me like I had crawled out of a dumpster. I'll never forget that mix of pity and condescension in his eyes. So I pushed it a little bit, trying to make a deal. I pulled out my checkbook and asked if for an extra five grand, I could just take Marvin home for the night. Not five grand to the zoo. Five grand to *him*."

Evie whistled. "Wow. You tried to bribe the zoo director. No wonder he was furious."

Gideon wilted. "And then when that didn't work, I threatened to cancel our donation."

Evie looked shocked. "You would do that?"

"I was obviously bluffing!" Gideon cried. "But he didn't fall for it." He put his head in his hands. "Now do you see why I couldn't tell Abby about it? She would think I was the world's biggest idiot. I honestly wonder sometimes why someone as amazing as her would ever want to be with me."

"You're not the only one," Evie muttered.

"So, just to recap here," Zach interjected, "you and Dr. Chang have an argument about whether or not you could keep Marvin. You then try to bribe him to let you take Marvin home for a night. Then you threaten the zoo. And then, coincidentally"—Zach hit heavy on the word *coincidentally*—"he goes missing that same night, huh? Interesting."

"And let's not forget you were completely alone for the exact window of time that Marvin was kidnapped," Vishal added. "So that gives you a *huge* motive and no alibi."

Gideon leveled his gaze at the three accusers, and

when he spoke, his voice was razor-sharp. "Are you forgetting that I was driven to the zoo entrance by a docent? She dropped me right at my car and saw me get in. Ask her if you'd like. Her name is Robin." He folded his arms across his chest. "And if that's not enough for you brats, you can check the security footage. It will show that I never came back into the zoo. That should be enough of an alibi."

"You could have driven your car out of sight and hopped the fence," Zach said. "No one would have seen you."

"But I didn't," Gideon insisted. "And I can prove it. Do you remember what I was wearing to the donor dinner?"

Zach's face fell. He knew where this was going. "A white suit."

"Exactly," Gideon said. "A white suit. If I hopped the fence, broke into Marvin's exhibit, and somehow managed to hop back over the fence carrying him, my perfect white suit would have been a mess. Did Abby mention anything about my clothes being dirty when I picked her up?" He shoved his phone at them. "Here. Call her and ask."

Zach pushed the phone to Evie, and she stepped out of the room. A few moments later, she returned and handed back Gideon's phone. "He's telling the truth," she said.

"I told you I was innocent," Gideon insisted. "So why don't you kids quit harassing me and let me get back to work?" He waved his hand dismissively at the door. "Besides," he sneered, "if I really wanted a red panda that bad, I could just buy one on the internet."

"What are you talking about?" Evie asked. "That's illegal."

"Is it?" Gideon pulled up a website. "See for yourself."

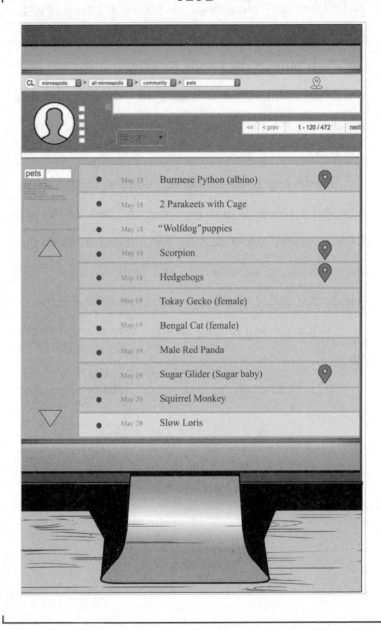

# CHAPTER
## 15

The three friends sat huddled together on the bus, talking quietly about the classified ad Gideon had shown them. "That illegal website has a red panda listed for sale, and the posting date is the day after Marvin disappeared!" Vishal said. "The panda in the ad has to be him!"

"So Marvin wasn't kidnapped because somebody wanted him; he was kidnapped for *money*," Evie said with disgust. Just wait until Sophia heard about this.

"We have to tell the police," Zach said.

"You're right," Evie said. "Call Detective Bermudez and let him know we're on our way." She pulled out her own phone. "But there's someone else who needs to hear this, too."

***

Sophia was in bed, blankets wrapped around her like a shroud, and streaming old detective shows when she heard her phone buzz. She dug through the mountain of throw pillows and fished it out to check the screen. Evie was calling. Sophia almost answered it, but instead she shoved the phone back under the pillows and let it go to voice mail.

Sophia had always been a confident person. An only child, she had spent her life around her parents and their sophisticated friends; she had never been one of those kids who was shy around adults, shunted off and relegated to some kids table at the holidays. Sure, she hadn't played with many children her own age, but she'd never really noticed. Sophia hadn't much liked the girls at her old school, but it wasn't like she was a kid who sat alone at lunch or anything like that, and she kept herself busy with activities and art classes the rest of the time. Sophia would never have considered herself a lonely person.

But then she'd met Vishal and the twins. Suddenly there was a whole new world of texts and adventures and inside jokes with them. She had become a part of something, and she liked feeling as though she belonged. She didn't just have someone to sit with at lunch; she had *friends* to sit with. Best friends.

Or so she thought.

But then she saw the look of surprise on Evie's and Zach's faces when she called them her best friends. The twins had recovered quickly enough, but whenever Sophia thought of that moment, she felt such a sharp pang of embarrassment that she wanted to twist into herself and squeeze the memory of it out of her head forever. She should have known better. After all, they were always yelling at her, telling her she was being rude or acting like a spoiled brat. They obviously didn't really like her. Why had she said such a stupid, stupid thing?

The phone buzzed again. It was Evie calling a second time. The pull to answer it was strong, but Sophia couldn't bring herself to. What could she say, anyway? At least if she was a good detective, they might want to keep her around. But practically every idea she'd had about the case was wrong. She was wrong about Jersey.

She was wrong about Abby. Wrong, wrong, wrong. Just like in their last case.

Evie switched to texting. Sophia heard the chime and told herself not to read it. There was a second chime, and she couldn't help herself. Had they solved the case without her?

HUGE NEWS! HEADING TO POLICE STATION

Sophia's stomach sank. They obviously had. She really wouldn't have expected it to be Gideon; he didn't seem the type to plan a theft that complicated. Plus, he was wearing a white suit that night. What kind of dummy would wear a white suit to commit a crime like that? It would have gotten filthy. She was curious in spite of herself. Her phone chimed again.

Meet u there?

Sophia wanted to go. She really did. Maybe they had already found Marvin. Maybe she would get to see him returned to the zoo. That would be nice. She picked up her phone.

But then she would have to sit and listen to how the Gemini Detective Agency cracked the case without her. They would all be laughing together, sharing that moment when, without her there to interfere, they realized the true solution to the mystery. Ugh. No thanks.

Sorry can't make it

Congrats!

???

CAN U JUST PLEASE COME WE NEED UR HELP

A glimmer of hope rose in Sophia's chest. Maybe they hadn't solved the case after all? They needed her help? She tapped out one last text.

On my way

Sophia leapt out of bed and grabbed her shoes. "Edgar!" she shouted as she ran down the stairs. "We need to get to the police station!"

***

Sophia burst through the police station's front door at a

full-on run, but stopped short when she saw Vishal and the twins waiting on the reception area's hard wooden benches. "Oh. Hi." She smoothed her hair and looked down at the floor, trying to seem like someone who always came bursting into buildings, and definitely *not* like a person who was just really excited to see her friends and hoped that someday they would like her as much as she liked them.

"Are you okay?" Zach asked. "You ran through the door like there was some kind of emergency."

So much for that. Sophia tried for a casual laugh that sounded more like a dying turkey. "Oh, you know what they say. Crime is always in a hurry, so we should be, too!" She literally had no idea what she was talking about.

"I've never heard that, have you?" Vishal said to the twins. They shrugged and shook their heads.

"Me neither," a voice said from behind the counter. Sophia recognized the round-bellied cop who had been at the desk when they had visited the station a few months earlier. He was painstakingly pecking away at an ancient computer keyboard, just like last time. Sophia wondered if he was still working on the same report.

"Uh, I think it was in a . . . *New Yorker* article I read once." Her parents had a stack of those magazines piled under a coffee table, but she'd never seen anyone actually reading them. "Anyhoo, what's up?" Sophia cringed inwardly as soon as the words came out of her mouth. When in her life had she ever said *anyhoo*? That's the kind of thing the regular Sophia would make fun of mercilessly.

Evie gave her a strange look, like she was going to ask her something but then thought better of it. "We're just waiting for Detective Bermudez. He should be out in a few minutes."

"Cool, cool." Sophia sat beside her, fully aware that the facade of casual nonchalance she thought she could carry had utterly unraveled at her feet. "So it wasn't Gideon, then, after all?"

"Nope," Evie said. "It turns out he did have a huge motive and solid opportunity, but he didn't do it."

"How do you know?" Sophia asked.

"Well, for one thing, his white suit was still spotless when he picked up Abby."

"Totally makes sense." Sophia smiled in spite of herself. At least she wasn't wrong all the time. "What else did you learn?"

Evie filled her in on everything they had discovered, with Zach and Vishal jumping in for some dramatic reenactments from time to time. Sophia found herself laughing when Vishal told her that the whole interrogation had almost fallen apart until Zach had saved the day with his little notebook.

"I was sitting there, sweating bullets because it was going nowhere fast, and then Zach jumps in like some kind of *professional* asking all these detailed questions." Vishal slapped Zach on the shoulder. "Dude, it was sick! How did you do it?"

Zach shrugged. "Well, while you were all busy winging it and flopping all over Gideon's couch, I used that time to make a plan. You know, like how I *tried* to do before you ditched me in the elevator and made me run after you?"

Vishal grimaced. "Fair point."

"Sounds like classic police strategy." Detective Bermudez's broad shoulders filled the doorway. He wore dark slacks and a blue Oxford with the sleeves rolled up, his coppery forearms bulging with muscles.

The group followed him along the winding cubicle path to his desk. Zach expected to see his bulletin board full of evidence of Marvin's kidnapping, but then he remembered that the city still thought the culprit was B-17. Instead the board was covered with photos of some artwork and a Fabergé egg. Boring. Well, all that would change as soon as they told him everything they had uncovered.

A short time later, after they had told their tale, the four young investigators stared at Detective Bermudez in surprise. "What do you mean, you don't think there's anything you can do? Don't you believe us?" Zach asked.

"Of course I believe you," Detective Bermudez said. "And I didn't say I couldn't do *anything*; we can notify Animal Control and the Department of Natural Resources about the website you found. They'll follow up on the ads, try to find the buyers, and get the site shut down. But as for Marvin's disappearance, we're in a tough spot. The zoo's official stance is that Marvin was killed by B-17. They haven't filed a report of theft, and until they do, there's nothing for police to investigate."

"Fine, then. I'd like to report a theft," Sophia said. Her lips were a thin line. "What do I need to fill out?"

"I'm afraid it doesn't work that way." The detective's voice was soft. "Unfortunately, only the owner of the missing property can report it stolen."

"But Marvin isn't property!" Sophia said.

"I understand that, but a red panda isn't a human being, so they are considered property according to Minnesota law."

Sophia folded her arms and glared. "So, that's it, then? It's just tough luck for us, and tough luck for Marvin? You're just going to let the kidnapper get away with it? You're not even following up on the website yourself! You're just making some call. Big deal; I could have done that on my own!"

Evie could see Detective Bermudez was trying hard to be patient. "I *have* to call the other departments, because they're the ones who investigate animal crimes. That's how the law works."

"But cops do investigate kidnapping, don't they?

Marvin was kidnapped, and you still aren't going to do anything about it, just because Marvin's an animal and not a person."

"Chill, Sophia. He's not saying that," Vishal said. He eyed the detective. "Are you?"

"I want to help you," Detective Bermudez said, "but animal-related crimes aren't under my jurisdiction, and I can't start an investigation into the theft without a formal complaint from the zoo. And the city council is putting a lot of pressure on every department about B-17. Folks are getting pretty worked up about having a wild bobcat roaming through the city. Some pets have gone missing, including Councilman Brown's own Yorkie, Peaches. Now the man is out for blood."

"That explains the press conference," Zach said grimly.

"Where did the pets go missing?" Evie asked.

"From all over the Twin Cities, but mostly Kenwood and Summit Hill."

"But that's not even B-17's territory," Sophia protested.

"Listen, I have to do what my boss orders me to

do," the detective said. "But I'll tell you what: Tell the zoo what you told me. Lay out your evidence. If you can convince the director to file a theft report with us, then I'll have the power to open an investigation. But until that happens, my hands are tied."

"And what about the red panda on the website?" Vishal asked.

"I will make sure that DNR and Animal Control make it their highest priority. If you can pass along any photos of Marvin you might have, they might be able to use them to compare to the panda in the ad." He stood up and led them back down the hall to the station entrance. "Assuming anyone can tell red pandas apart. I have a feeling they all look the same."

"Yup," Vishal agreed. "All equally adorable."

As they stopped to say goodbye, Vishal noticed a bulletin board plastered with photos. "Are those the missing pets?" he asked. The detective nodded. Vishal took a closer look. "Huh," he said.

"What?" Evie asked.

"Well, if B-17 is responsible for all of these, she must have really expensive taste."

# CHAPTER
# 16

Vishal sat in the back of the Boyds' black SUV, researching the animals in the photos he had snapped of the bulletin board at the police station. "Those missing pets are all rare or fancy breeds," he said. "Did you know that a Tibetan mastiff puppy recently sold for over a million dollars?"

"One million dollars for a puppy? Why would anyone pay all that money when they could just adopt one from a shelter for almost nothing?" Evie asked.

Zach shook his head. "I will never understand rich people."

"Hey!" Sophia elbowed him. "I'm sitting right here, you know! And, BTW, I would never get a dog from a breeder. So don't lump me in with them!"

"Sorry," Zach said sheepishly. "I wasn't talking about you."

"Can I see that map again?" Evie asked. She studied it for a moment. "These pets are from all over the Twin Cities. There's no way this could all be B-17."

"Well, duh," Sophia said. "How's a wild bobcat going to catch a python? It's not like someone lets their pet snake just hang out in the backyard; those things live in heated terrariums. What did B-17 do? Disguise herself as the maid and talk her way into the house?"

"Do you think the missing pets are related to Marvin's disappearance?" Zach asked.

"Good question," Evie answered. "My guess would be no. I mean, Marvin went missing from the zoo, and the others were from private homes."

"But it seems like a pretty big coincidence that all of these animals disappeared around the same time," Vishal said.

Zach pulled out his notebook and jotted something down. "We should check pet sale websites and see if the animals for sale fit any of the descriptions from the flyers."

"Good idea," Vishal said as Edgar pulled up in front of his house. "I'll start searching after I finish my homework."

"Cool," Evie said. "Back to the zoo tomorrow?" The others nodded. "I just hope we can convince the director to listen to us."

"Don't worry," Sophia said. "If there's one person we can count on, it's Dr. Chang."

***

Dr. Chang stacked a pile of papers on his desk and tucked them into a workbag, keeping one eye on the clock. "I know you children mean well," he said, "but I have a fund-raising meeting in an hour, and with this latest round of budget cuts, I need to focus every ounce of attention on keeping the zoo open. I simply don't have time to listen to conspiracy theories about a red panda that we already know was eaten by a bobcat."

"But surely you can't still believe that's what happened to Marvin," Zach said. "What about all the evidence we showed you?"

"An empty meat container and an exotic pet website is hardly enough to go on," the zoo director said.

"B-17 was in the vicinity of the zoo that night, and we found her paw print inside the red panda exhibit. Quite frankly, it's an open-and-shut case."

"It is if you ignore everything that doesn't fit your theory," Sophia snapped.

"I know that it might be hard to accept what happened to our red panda, Sophia. Your parents told me of your work with MEOWS, so I understand why you want to believe that the bobcat isn't responsible. But wishful thinking won't bring Marvin back."

"But what if it isn't wishful thinking?" Vishal asked. "What if we're right?" The zoo director just shook his head.

"Fine," Evie said. "I understand you're busy and you don't want to investigate. Can you at least help us investigate it on our own? Did any of the donors at the dinner try to back out of their pledges? Anyone say they were short on cash?"

Dr. Chang sighed wearily. "You know that all donor information is strictly confidential."

"Please, there must be something you can do," Zach said. "If not for Marvin, for B-17. The city council vote is this Monday, and if they follow through with Brown's plan, she'll die. It's not just unfair; it's *wrong*!" Zach was surprised at the vehemence in his own voice.

"I agree with you on that point," Dr. Chang said. "B-17 has as much a right to live here as we do, and it's our job to learn to adapt to her, just as she has learned to adapt to us."

"Then *do* something about it," Sophia said. "Help us prove her innocence!"

Dr. Chang stood up and tucked his bag under his arm. "I'm sorry, but I can't help prove something that isn't true."

Sophia was almost in tears. "Dr. Chang, I don't understand why you won't listen to us. You're the one person I thought would really care about making things right."

The zoo director didn't answer. Without making eye contact with any of them, he walked to the doorway. "If you'll excuse me, I have a fund-raising meeting to attend." Disappointed and bewildered, the others stood up. Dr. Chang was already halfway down the hall; he never looked back.

"I thought Dr. Chang would be on our side," Sophia said bleakly. "What just happened?"

Evie pointed at something on the zoo director's desk. "Maybe there's a reason he doesn't want Marvin found."

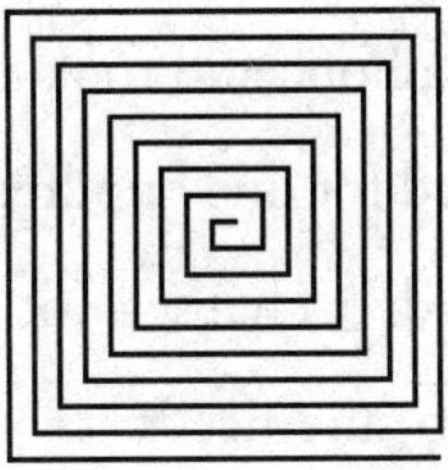

# CHAPTER
# 17

"That's an insurance claim form for Marvin," Evie said. She pulled out her phone and took a photo of the form. "Marvin was insured for one hundred thousand dollars."

Vishal whistled. "That's a lot of money, and it sounds like the zoo sure needs it."

"But would Dr. Chang really kidnap one of the zoo's animals just for the insurance money?" Zach asked.

"Not just the insurance money, remember? There's also the money he'd get for selling Marvin on the black market." Evie waited for Sophia to interrupt her and defend Dr. Chang, but she was silent. "Dr. Chang would never do that, though, right, Sophia? I mean, he's the zoo director."

Sophia walked into the hall, and the others

followed. "If you'd asked me yesterday, I would never have dreamed that he could be a suspect," she said quietly. "But he was so *strange* just then. It wasn't only that he didn't listen to us; it was like he didn't even *want* to listen." She lowered her voice even more. "Honestly, I don't know who to trust anymore."

"Well if it is him, then we'll have to work even harder to prove it," Zach said. "Maybe we should follow up on the website angle. After all, who knows how long the DNR or Animal Control will take to start investigating it? We can answer the ad ourselves and set up a meeting. When the kidnapper shows up, we'll catch him in the act."

A slow smile spread on Vishal's face. "That could actually work. We need to set up a dummy email account first, though. Is there a computer we could use here?"

"There's one in the volunteer center," Sophia suggested.

*** 

A short time later, the four looked approvingly at the message they had composed under their new fake account, pandafan365: *Hi. I saw your ad for the red panda, and I'm very interested. I work in cash only. Let's meet.*

"I like it," Vishal said. "Short, sweet, and to the point."

"I still think it could use more backstory, but it gets the job done," Sophia agreed.

Evie pointed at the little Sent icon next to the message. "There it goes. Now what?"

"Now we wait for the kidnapper to write back," Zach said.

"Ugh, I hate waiting," Sophia said. "Isn't there something we can do in the meantime?"

"What about those photos of Marvin for Detective Bermudez?" Evie suggested. "The zoo has a photographer, right?"

Sophia nodded. "Lester Pham. I think I know where his office is." She led them out into the zoo to a wooden building near the giraffe enclosure. Vishal let out an enchanted squeal when he spied a baby giraffe cuddling close to its mother. "Look at the baby! So little!"

Sophia laughed. "Baby giraffes are six feet tall when they're born, but sure, I guess you could call her little." The group paused to watch the mother nuzzle her young baby for a moment before they went inside to Lester's office.

The photographer's work space was part studio and part library. Photographs of animals covered every available wall space, and the L-shaped desk had several large monitors and a high-tech printer. Lester bent over a monitor, peering intently at an image of a tall, crowned bird. "Hi, Lester," Sophia said.

Lester looked up. "Hey, Sophia. What's new?"

"Not much," Sophia said. She introduced her friends.

"Oh, yeah," Lester said, "I recognize you from the donor dinner. Do you volunteer with Sophia?"

"No, but I'd like to," Evie replied. "We helped out the other day, and it was really fun."

"You should do it," Lester said. "I started out here as a volunteer when I was your age. Now I have my dream job; I get to spend all day taking pictures of animals."

"That's pretty cool," Zach said. "What's your

favorite animal to photograph?"

"That's a hard one," Lester answered. "I think my favorite pictures are when I capture an animal in an unexpected way that makes people look at it differently." He pointed to a framed photograph of an adult alligator with a tiny baby riding on its snout. "Like this one. This is an alligator giving one of her babies a ride. People think of alligators as dangerous predators, but they're also great mothers. They take very tender care of their young."

"I didn't know that," Vishal said. His eyes ran over the wall of photographs. He pointed to one. "Is that Marvin?"

Lester nodded sadly. "I took that a few years ago."

"Do you have any more recent photos that you could print out for us?" Sophia asked. "It's for a project."

"Of course." Lester opened up a folder and selected a few images for printing. "It will just take a few minutes. Do you want to see some of the pics from the donor dinner in the meantime? I think I got some great ones of you with Shakti, and a few with Billy the elephant, too."

Vishal looked at Zach with a smirk. "I think Zach would love a picture of himself with Shakti. Maybe you could put it in a heart-shaped frame for him?"

The others laughed, and Zach grinned and puffed out his chest. "Vishal's just jealous because Shakti liked me better."

"She's pretty special, isn't she?" Lester asked.

"The best rhino in the world," Zach agreed. "I mean, I've never met any others, but you can just tell."

"I get it," Lester said. "Here." He pulled out a stack of photos. "I printed out a bunch of pictures to send out to the dinner attendees. Feel free to sort through them and find some you like. I just need to get my other memory stick from the car. I'll be back in a few minutes."

The kids leafed through the photos while they waited. There was an image of a grinning Vishal feeding rose petals to Prudence the sloth. Another of Sophia and her parents talking to a leather-gauntleted keeper with an owl perched on her wrist. And a particularly sweet one of the twins stroking Shakti's snout with wonder in their eyes. They quickly sifted through photos taken throughout the night, hoping to find one of the four of them together. Suddenly, Zach let out a tiny exclamation, and the photos in his hand dropped to the floor. "What is it?" Evie asked.

Zach sorted back through the photos and laid out a few on the table. "I know how Marvin was stolen, and I know who did it."

# CHAPTER

## 18

Zach pointed to a photo of Dante and Bitsy taken later in the night. They were sitting in one of the carts next to a docent holding Prudence the sloth. Bitsy was smiling brightly, but a small bead of sweat was trickling down her forehead. "I still don't know why she would wear that awful coat; it wasn't even cold that night," Sophia said with disgust. "No wonder she was so overheated."

Zach pointed at Bitsy's collar. "Look more closely."

Sophia gasped. "Oh, my gosh, Zach. You genius! No wonder she wore that stupid coat!" Nestled around Bitsy's neck and tucked under the collar of her fox-fur coat was a sleeping Marvin. Sophia could see his snout peeping out near her collarbone.

"She must have fed Marvin with drugged meat,"

Vishal said. "It makes total sense. She wouldn't have to worry about a carrier or coming back for him. She could just walk right out of the zoo with him draped around her neck." His voice held grudging admiration. "I hate to say it, but it's a pretty brilliant plan."

Evie nodded her head slowly. "It is. But I still can't believe *Bitsy* did it. I had her pegged as a total ditz!"

"Ditzy Bitsy," Sophia agreed. "I didn't even think she cared about animals. I guess she has hidden depths." Suddenly her expression changed. "Oh, no. What if it's one of those Cruella de Vil situations? What if she stole Marvin for his fur?"

"We have to tell Detective Bermudez right away," Zach said. "We have all the evidence; now the police can arrest her and get Marvin back."

"Should we tell the zoo first?" Vishal asked.

Sophia shook her head. "No time. We don't know where Marvin is or how he's being cared for. I doubt Bitsy even knows anything about red pandas. The longer he's gone, the greater the danger he's in."

Evie snapped a picture of the photo of Bitsy and texted it to Detective Bermudez along with the details of the crime. Her phone rang seconds later. She listened for a few moments. "Okay. We'll be right there." She hung up and turned to the others. "He wants us to meet him at the station."

"Edgar's on his way to pick us up," Sophia said. She scooped up the photos of Bitsy, and they rushed to the doorway, bumping into Lester, who had just returned.

"Hey, I found these great shots of Marvin I took last summer!" His expression turned to confusion when he saw the look of urgency on the four detectives' faces. "Is everything all right? What's happening?"

The kids broke into a run. "No time to explain," Vishal called over his shoulder. "Thanks for the photos!"

\*\*\*

Detective Bermudez was in the station's conference room briefing a small team of police and animal control officers. "The suspect's name is Bitsy Romanevsky. She is a female with blond hair and brown eyes. Mid- to late twenties, petite, approximately five feet two inches tall. We've secured a warrant to search the suspect's address at 120 Eighth Avenue North, in the North Loop. She may or may not have the red panda in her possession at this time." He looked up and saw the kids. "Oh, good, you're here. Do you have the photos with you?"

Evie wordlessly handed over the pictures. He quickly sifted through them and passed them around. He handed a close-up photo of Bitsy to a young officer. "Could you please make some copies of this so everyone knows what the suspect looks like?" The officer hurried off. "Thanks for coming in," he said before introducing them to the group. There were a few snickers in the room when he described the kids as junior detectives, but a quick look silenced them. "Zach and Evie are Yaro's kids," Bermudez added, and the police officers' faces grew somber. "Those of you who have been around long enough to remember Yaro know what an honor it was to work with such a dedicated cop." There were nods in the room.

Zach squeezed his sister's hand. "I wish Dad was here to see this," he whispered.

"Me too," Evie whispered back.

Bermudez clapped his hands together. "All right, team. Let's move out."

The police and animal control officers headed out the door, and Bermudez led the teens down the hallway to an unmarked van with a young plainclothes officer behind the wheel. The detective hopped into the front passenger seat, and the kids climbed into the back. He twisted around in his seat to face them. "Your job today is to *stay in the van*. We don't have any background on Bitsy. We don't know if she's working alone or has an accomplice, and that creates a potentially hazardous situation. You're here solely to identify her, got it? So promise you'll stay in the van until I come and get you."

Evie bit her lip. This was all happening so fast, and it felt much more real and frightening than she had thought it would. In their previous case they were mostly on their own, so being scared made sense. But she had expected to feel braver with a bunch of adults around. "We promise."

The van arrived in Bitsy's neighborhood and parked several blocks away from her apartment. Bermudez hopped out of the van, paperwork in hand, and joined the other officers on the walk over to Bitsy's apartment. Evie folded her hands in her lap and tried to think calming, positive thoughts, but anxiety kept creeping in. Evie could feel the tension as they waited for the crackle of the radio that would tell them that Bitsy had been captured and Marvin was safe. But the van was silent.

"What's taking so long?" Sophia whispered to Evie. "Do you think something happened?"

Evie's stomach sank. She took a deep breath, willing her hammering heart to slow down. She leaned forward. "Excuse me, ma'am?"

The driver turned around and smiled. "I'm Officer Cho." She put out her hand, and Evie shook it. "What's up?"

"I was just wondering," Evie said, "is Detective Bermudez in any danger?"

"Well, any unknown situation can be dangerous, but Bermudez is good police. He's calm, he's professional, and he always keeps his cool. Don't worry."

Don't worry? The kids all looked at one another. There were a million different things that could go wrong. How were they not supposed to worry?

"I thought this would feel exciting," Evie whispered to her brother, "but sitting here waiting in the van is way worse than being in there ourselves. I keep wondering what's happening and thinking of all the things that could go wrong."

"Mom said that one of the reasons she became a crime reporter was because she couldn't stand sitting at home worrying every time Dad went to work."

Just then, Officer Cho's radio crackled to life. After a few garbled exchanges, she turned back to the kids. "All clear," she said. "We're going in."

"Did they find Marvin?" Sophia asked. Officer Cho shook her head, and Sophia slumped.

"Don't give up hope," Vishal said. "I'm sure the cops will find him." As they approached the apartment building, he expected to see Bitsy in handcuffs, maybe in the back of the police car or sitting on the curb. "Where is she?" he asked.

Bermudez's face was weary when the kids found him in the hallway outside of Bitsy's apartment. He carried a small spiral notebook and a pen. "What do you know about Ms. Romanevsky's background?" he asked them.

"Not much," Zach answered. "We only met her that one time at the donor dinner. She was mostly glommed onto her boyfriend, Dante, hanging onto his every word."

"What's Dante's last name?" Bermudez asked, his pen at the ready.

"Fishman," Vishal answered. "He's a game developer; he's working with Gideon Doheny." He leaned forward and tried to peer into the apartment through the open doorway. "Why all the questions? Isn't Bitsy talking?"

Bermudez shook his head. "She can't."

Sophia's eyes bulged. "What do you mean she can't? Is she dead?" She pushed forward. "Where's the body? Can I see it?"

"Easy, Morticia," Evie said. "Let's maybe wait until we have the whole story before you go all *Forensic Files* on us."

"Settle down, everyone," Bermudez said. "Ms. Romanevsky isn't dead; she just isn't here,"

"Well, she'll be back at some point, won't she?" Sophia asked.

"It's hard to say," Bermudez said, "The apartment doesn't give us much to go on. I'll have officers contact her boyfriend to see where she might be. In the meantime, I thought you could help me check and see if there are any clues we might be overlooking."

The detective handed out gloves, and everyone pulled on a pair before he led them inside. The animal control officers were kneeling over their equipment as they packed up to leave. "There's no evidence that a red panda was here," one officer said. "No evidence of any animals, in fact." Zach felt a trickle of doubt run through his veins. Had he been wrong about Bitsy?

Several police officers were still searching the apartment, but their faces didn't leave much room for hope. "There's nothing much here," said a short man with a shining, bald head. "Almost nothing personal of any kind. No photos, no notes or letters. Even the trash cans are empty." Zach looked around the sterile apartment. White walls, beige carpet, and the standard vertical blinds. The kitchen looked like it had never been used, and the furniture was straight out of a showroom. Tasteful, generic knickknacks were scattered artfully along the otherwise empty shelves. Even the perfectly coordinated throw pillows were pristinely fluffed and positioned.

"Does anyone even sit on this couch ever?" Vishal asked. He ran his finger along a tabletop. Not a speck of dust. "How long has she lived here, anyway?"

"According to the lease, Ms. Romanevsky's been here about four months," Bermudez answered.

"Why would someone who's lived in town for only four months want to steal Marvin?" Sophia asked.

Zach felt his doubts deepen. "Maybe . . ." he said. His voice grew smaller. "Maybe I messed up?" What if it hadn't been Marvin inside her coat? "I shouldn't have rushed it. I should have been more careful before we called you," he said to the detective.

Bermudez put his hand on Zach's shoulder. "Hey, it was my call to go in. You did the right thing."

"Listen, Zach, don't beat yourself up," Sophia said.

"I know. Everyone makes mistakes and all that. It's just—"

"No, that's not what I mean," Sophia interrupted. "Don't beat yourself up because you didn't make a mistake." She pointed across the room. "See? You were right."

# CHAPTER
# 19

"I'll bet anything that's what she used to make that fake bobcat print to frame B-17," Sophia said, pointing to the paw-print relief sculpture on the shelf. "If you look carefully, I'm sure you'll find there's still some sand residue from Marvin's exhibit."

Bermudez pulled out a magnifier and scanned the sculpture. Vishal elbowed Zach. "Check it," he whispered. "Sherlock Holmes style!" Zach grinned.

Bermudez looked up. "There are small grains of something on here." He carefully bagged and labeled the sculpture and handed it off to another officer. "Bring this to the lab and ask them to check for a match to the sand from the red panda exhibit." The officer hurried off.

Bitsy's bedroom was every bit as sterile as the rest of the apartment. The neatly made bed looked like it had never been slept in, the sheets still crisp like they had just come out of the box. A few of Bitsy's slinky dresses hung in the closet, along with the fox-fur coat. "That's the coat she was wearing when she took Marvin," Evie cried.

There was a commotion out in the hallway. "What's going on? Why can't I come in?" a voice demanded. One of the officers answered something in low, calming tones, and the voice rose higher. "But I'm her boyfriend!"

"It's Dante!" Evie whispered. They rushed out after Detective Bermudez to find the game developer standing in the doorway, his linen pants wrinkled and his curly hair wild.

"What are the cops doing here?" Dante demanded. "Where is she?"

"That's what we'd like to ask you," the detective answered. "When did you last see her?"

"Not since the night of the zoo dinner." He pointed at the kids. "Hey, you were there, too! Why are you in my girlfriend's apartment?"

"It's for a school project," Sophia said quickly. She had discovered that adults would buy pretty much anything if you said it was for a school project. Apparently it worked, because Dante nodded his head slowly as if that made perfect sense. Bermudez seemed to understand that the kids would get more out of Dante than he would, so he leaned against the wall, his dark eyes watching to see how the conversation would unfold.

"It looked like you guys were having an awesome time the other night at the zoo," Zach said with a smile. "How great was that rhino?"

Dante shrugged. "I thought the rhino was pretty beast, but Bitsy didn't seem that psyched about it. I guess she wasn't feeling well, because she ran off to the bathroom as soon as we got back to the party, and she was in there for, like, twenty minutes. She wanted to leave right after that, and hey, I get it. There's nothing worse than trying to party when your guts aren't down, if you know what I mean. I felt really bad for her. She was all flushed and sweaty, but she kept talking about how cold she was and huddling up in her coat."

Zach and Evie looked at each other. *Bingo.* "Did

184

you drive her home after that?" Zach asked.

"No, she had a client meeting right beforehand, so she had her own car. The docent brought the cart right to Bitsy's parking spot and she got in and drove off." He frowned at the memory. "She barely even said good night."

"Yeah, being sick is the worst, right?" Sophia said. "So you said she had a client meeting? What kind of work does she do?"

Dante waved his hand vaguely. "Some kind of sales and marketing thing, I don't really know."

"You don't know what your girlfriend does for a living?" Vishal asked incredulously.

"It's not like I didn't ask," Dante said defensively. "She didn't really like to talk about work."

"So what did you guys talk about?" Sophia asked.

Dante thought for a moment. "Me, mostly. She loved hearing about my work, and she said she knew Monkeyfarts Mayhem would be a huge hit; she had all these great suggestions to make it really epic. It was actually her idea to donate to the zoo and try to get the whole naming thing going. Gideon was crazy about the idea. It would be so boss to have an actual Monkeyfarts Manor exhibit! I still don't know why Dr. Chang wouldn't go for it."

Sophia rolled her eyes. "Yeah, what's wrong with that guy?" she asked, barely able to contain her sarcasm.

"That's cool that Bitsy wanted to help launch your app," Zach said. "Were you guys dating a long time?"

"At least a couple months, I guess," Dante answered. He thought for a moment. "We met around the end of January, so probably about four months."

"How did you meet?" Evie asked.

"I was out one night with a bunch of my investors, and one of the guys was ribbing me about how I always date blondes. I guess Bitsy overheard the convo, because she came right over and teased me about it. We just really hit it off right from the start, I guess."

Evie's eyes narrowed. Bitsy just *happens* to strike up a conversation with Dante? And then she just *happens* to give Dante the idea that gets him in with the zoo? *Sounds like a setup to me,* Evie thought. She snuck a glance at Detective Bermudez. His eyes glittered with interest, and his pen hovered over his open notebook.

"Have you been to Ms. Romanevsky's apartment much?" Bermudez asked.

Dante looked disconcerted for a moment, as though he had forgotten the police were even in the room. "What's with all the questions, anyway? Where's Bitsy?" he asked again.

Sophia gritted her teeth, trying to hide her frustration. Just when Dante was starting to spill the really interesting stuff, Bermudez had to go and ruin it. They were never going to find Marvin at this rate! She made her best puppy-dog eyes. "We were supposed to meet Bitsy at her apartment for our school project, and when she didn't show up we got really worried, so we called the police." She batted her eyelashes. "Were you supposed to meet her here, too?" Sophia doubted her little performance would work, but she was desperate. She cringed as soon as the words left her mouth; anyone could see it was obviously a lie.

To Sophia's surprise, Dante accepted her story without question. "That's a bummer she didn't show up when she said she'd meet you guys, but she has been acting kind of weird lately."

"Weird?" Zach asked. "Like how?"

Dante ran his hand through his curls, making them stick out from his head like dandelion fluff. "Well, the morning after the zoo party, I called to see if she was feeling better, and she said she was still doing pretty rotten but she'd call me later. I didn't hear from her, and then two days later she dumped me!"

"So you came over here to try to get her back?" Sophia asked. She hadn't pegged Dante for a romantic.

"No, I came to get my pinkie ring."

Sophia blinked. "Your pinkie ring?"

"Yeah," Dante explained. "I was getting ready to go out tonight and I noticed my diamond pinkie ring was missing. The last time I saw it was when I was with Bitsy, so I thought she might know where it is." He sighed. "I'm always losing stuff around her: my platinum cufflinks, my money clip, and now my ring. Man, I guess I'm just so happy with her I get super-forgetful, you know?"

"No, yeah, sure," Sophia said. Wow. It never once occurred to Dante that Bitsy might have been ripping him off? *Man, if he's really this dumb, he's going to be hit with a lot of bad news all at once,* Sophia thought. Out loud she said, "Hey, Detective Bermudez, do your officers want to help Dante search for his pinkie ring?"

The detective gave a brisk nod, and the police fanned out, opening empty drawers and cabinets, searching for any clue that might help them learn more about Bitsy or why she would go to so much trouble to steal a red panda. "Was Bitsy's apartment always so . . . plain?" Vishal asked. He bent down and peered at a loose vent cover behind a credenza.

"I don't really know," Dante said. "We were mostly over at my place. But her pad does seem a little emptier than I remember."

Evie felt her worst suspicions confirmed. The apartment didn't feel like a place Bitsy had expected to be in for long, and if even clueless Dante thought it looked emptier than usual, it must mean that she had already cleared out. But how had Bitsy known the police were on her trail?

Detective Bermudez seemed to echo Evie's thoughts. "I'm afraid I have some bad news for you, Mr. Fishman. It appears Ms. Romanevsky may have absconded with your pinkie ring and a number of other missing items."

Dante's eyebrows knitted together in confusion. "She did *what*, now?"

"She took off," the detective said simply. "She's gone, and so is your stuff."

Dante looked stricken, and he leaned against the wall in support. "My girl? No way. Bitsy would never. She knows I loved that pinkie ring! And my cufflinks." His voice sank. "And my . . . money."

"Well, the good news is, with her flashy looks and a name like Bitsy Romanevsky, she won't be too hard to find again, right?" Zach asked hopefully.

Suddenly, Vishal let out a groan. "I wouldn't count on it," he said.

# CHAPTER
# 20

"Wait a minute, that's Bitsy's hair!" Dante cried, pointing at the blond wig that Vishal had found.

"And it looks like her blond hair wasn't the only fake thing about her," Vishal said. "Look at all these IDs! Each one has a different name, but they're all Bitsy's face."

"So Bitsy Romanevsky was just an alias," Sophia said in a whisper. "Then who is she really?"

"This case just got a lot bigger than we thought," Bermudez said. He turned to a young, bald policeman. "Sergeant Ring, would you please escort Mr. Fishman outside and take his statement?" A bewildered Dante meekly followed the sergeant out of the apartment. Bermudez turned to the four teens. "Kids, I'm sorry to say this, but this evidence gives me reason to believe Bitsy was a professional thief. We've spent the past year tracking the Cat's Paw, a burglar who's been working the Twin Cities. I now believe Bitsy and the Cat's Paw are one and the same."

"Our mom's written about the Cat's Paw!" Zach said. "She stole a Picasso from a mansion in Kenwood, a Fabergé egg from an auction house, and Babe Ruth's 1919 trade contract from a sports exhibit at the history museum. She always leaves a cat paw print behind as her calling card." His eyes widened. "Oh, no way! The print in Marvin's exhibit wasn't to frame B-17; it was her signature!"

Evie was incredulous. "Wait a minute. *Bitsy's* the Cat's Paw?" She shook her head. "There's just no way. The Cat's Paw is a master thief, and Bitsy's, well . . . kind of an airhead."

Sophia shook her head. "No; Ditzy Bitsy is who she wanted you to see. Everything about her was as fake as that wig."

"And I'm afraid that means that stealing the red panda was a hired job," Bermudez said. "She most likely handed him off to her employer the same night she took him. Thanks for all your help; you've given us a huge lead in the Cat's Paw case."

"But what about our case?" Sophia asked. "Are you still going to help us find Marvin?"

"I don't want *you* to try to find anyone, okay? The Cat's Paw has worked for some very dangerous people, so you need to let us take it from here." He gently ushered the kids out of the apartment. "Officer Cho is waiting downstairs to drive you home."

The kids found themselves standing alone in the long hallway, staring at a blank, white door.

"Wait, what just happened?" Evie asked.

"I have no idea," Vishal said.

"I do." Sophia wilted against the wall. "It means they'll probably never catch the real kidnappers. And we're still no closer to finding Marvin."

***

The next day at lunch Vishal and the twins poked listlessly at the food on their trays, and Sophia barely touched her California roll. "I don't understand it," Zach said. "We managed to prove that Marvin was kidnapped *and* identify the person who kidnapped him, but now we lost the only real lead we have?"

"Not to mention the city council is still planning to vote on destroying B-17 on Monday," Sophia said bitterly.

Evie dropped her spork in disgust. "But that's so unfair! We have proof that B-17 is innocent. Why aren't they showing it on the news? If people only knew the truth, they wouldn't let something like this happen!"

"Detective Bermudez said something about 'not wanting to compromise the investigation,' whatever that means," Zach said. "He said if the kidnappers figure out that we know Marvin wasn't really eaten, they'll go underground and then we may never find him."

"But if we don't get Marvin back in the next four days, you know how the city council is gonna vote on B-17," Evie said. "Sure, solving a case takes time, but that's time that little bobcat doesn't have."

Sophia rested her chin in her hand and picked at a scratch on the Formica tabletop. "All that work, and we're right back where we started: with absolutely nothing. And without Bitsy, we still have no idea who's really behind the kidnapping."

"Wait a minute," Vishal said. "We do still have one other lead." He pulled out his phone. "Remember? The red panda ad!"

Sophia lifted her head and a glint of interest flitted across her face. "Is the ad still up?"

"Let me see," Vishal said. He tapped the screen and shook his head. His shoulders slumped. "The whole website's gone. That means either the DNR and Animal Control shut it down, or the kidnappers got wind someone was onto them and shut it down themselves."

"So, basically it's either really good news or really bad news," Zach said.

"If Marvin wasn't found yet, then it can mean only bad news. Now we don't even have the ad to go on," Sophia said glumly.

"Hang on," Vishal said. "Let me check the email address we created. Maybe the kidnappers wrote back before the site was shut down." A few moments later he let out a high-pitched squeal of triumph. "Yesssss! It's here!"

The others crowded around the tiny screen. "I don't get it," Evie said. "All it says is 'Don't be afraid to wear your heart on your sleeve,' and then there's just a link."

Vishal tapped on the link, and the four kids were silent for a moment as they figured out what it meant. "Um," Vishal finally said, "do any of you know how to dance?"

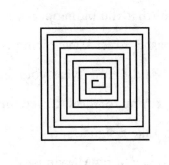

# CHAPTER
## 21

"This must mean that the kidnappers want to rendezvous at the Wabasha Street Cave Swing Night tonight at seven," Vishal said. "And 'wear your heart on your sleeve' must be a hint for how to let the kidnappers who to look for. Like a signal."

"Why would they bring Marvin to a crowded swing dance party?" Sophia asked. "Wouldn't he be noticed?"

"Not necessarily," Evie said. "In fifth grade we went on a guided tour of the caves, and they stretch way beyond the part with the restaurant and nightclub. The tour guide even showed us a part of a side cave where some squatters camped out for months without anyone knowing they were there."

"So the kidnappers could be holding Marvin in one

of the side caves without anyone finding them," Sophia said thoughtfully.

"Why not?" Vishal asked. "It would be a good hiding place. All we have to do is watch everyone at the swing dance and see if anyone sneaks away. Then we follow them to Marvin. Easy peasy!"

"Wait a second," Zach said. "There are about a million holes in this plan. First of all, there's no way four kids can just show up at Swing Night on our own. We'd stick out like a bunch of sore thumbs! And what if the person behind the kidnapping is someone who knows us, like Dr. Chang? We'll get recognized in a heartbeat! Plus the kidnappers are setting up a meeting, right? They're expecting to meet some adult who's ready to buy a red panda. If nobody shows, they're gonna get suspicious." He folded his arms. "I say we tell Detective Bermudez and have him go in undercover."

"Are you kidding?" Sophia asked. "After the way he just booted us off the case? *We* were the ones who put all the clues together, and he treated us like we were nothing but a bunch of kids."

"But we *are* a bunch of kids," Zach said. "Just

because we solved one case in our lives, it doesn't make us professional detectives. What if we screw up?"

"So what if we do?" Sophia shot back. "Adults screw up all the time, and nobody tells them to stay home. What makes them any better than us?" She shook her head. "Besides, somebody must have tipped off Bitsy and given her time to skip town before the cops arrived. And until we know who the leak is, we can't trust anyone in the police department. We don't want the kidnappers to get tipped off again and disappear before we find Marvin."

"I get what you're saying, but I think Zach's right," Evie said. "There's too much risk in going alone."

"Maybe we could convince our parents to pretend to be the buyers," Sophia suggested.

"Would yours do it?" Evie asked.

Sophia slumped. "Probably not. They would say the whole thing is way too dangerous."

"Mine, too," Vishal said.

"Yeah," Evie agreed. "Our mom may be a crime reporter, but she's still a mom. I think she'd rather keep us out of it."

"Exactly," Zach said. "And since none of our parents will agree to come along, we have no choice but to leave it to the professionals. That's the smart thing to do."

"There could be another option," Vishal said. "All we have to do is find an adult who looks like someone with money. Someone who seems like they would buy a red panda, right?"

"Uh-huh," Sophia agreed.

"And someone who wouldn't be all overprotective and say it's too dangerous for us to come along," Vishal continued.

"Yeah," Evie said, "but what reasonable adult would be like that?"

"Oh, I don't know," Vishal said casually. "I might be able to think of someone who matches that description."

Zach's face twisted with distaste as comprehension dawned on him. "Oh, no way, Vish. You can't be serious."

"Why not?" Vishal shot back.

"Well, for one thing he can't stand us," Zach said. "I'm telling you, there's absolutely no way he'd do it."

***

Gideon Doheny glowered at the four young detectives sitting across from him. "Let me get this straight. Not two days ago you were in this very office accusing me of Marvin's kidnapping, and now you walk in here to ask me to take you to the Wabasha Street Caves tonight?"

"And maybe do some dancing," Vishal added.

"And maybe do some dancing," Gideon repeated skeptically. "And why would I want to do that, exactly?"

"It's for a school project," Sophia said smoothly. She watched his face, waiting for the magic words to do their work.

Gideon's stony expression didn't change. "Listen, kid. Don't try to con me. I used that whole 'school project' line from second grade until I dropped out of college, okay?"

"I . . . I wasn't . . ." Sophia stammered, embarrassed to be caught in a lie. Her cheeks flushed bright pink.

Gideon held up his hand. "Save it." Sophia closed her mouth. "Look, if there's something you're trying to get from me, just give it to me straight. If I want to do it, I'll do it. Otherwise, you can quit wasting my time and tell your story walking."

"'Tell your story walking'?" Evie asked. "What does that mean?"

"It means get out of here! So spill it or get lost so I can get back to work."

The Gemini Detectives looked at one another. What would Gideon say if they told him the truth? Would he try to stop them? Call their parents? The others finally nodded at Sophia. They were running out of time, and for better or for worse, they had to take a risk. Sophia took a deep breath and spilled the whole story. When it was over, Gideon's face showed no expression. "So, will you do it?" Sophia finally asked.

"Quite frankly, I don't see why I should," Gideon said.

"What do you mean? You love red pandas! Don't you want to help Marvin?"

"If you're right about what's happening tonight, I could go on my own and buy Marvin myself. Why would I send him back to the zoo when I finally have the chance to own him as a pet?"

Sophia's voice was heated. "Because the zoo is Marvin's *home*! And if you love Marvin as much as you say you do, you wouldn't support him being kidnapped and given to people who don't know the first thing about caring for him. Do you know how many animals die because of the exotic pet trade? It's disgusting!"

Gideon shrugged. "Like I said, animal rights are Abby's thing, not mine."

Sophia was stunned into silence. Most adults she knew at least pretended to care about something besides themselves. She had never met a grown-up so unapologetically selfish before. She cast about desperately for something to say, but if Gideon wasn't willing to lift a finger even to save his favorite animal, she couldn't think of a single thing that would convince him to change his mind.

Vishal tried another angle. He smiled and made his voice light and casual. "So, how are things with Abby these days?"

Gideon grimaced. "She's still pretty steamed about the whole zoo thing, and she wants me to stop helping Big Tommy run for mayor." He shrugged helplessly. "But what am I supposed to do? The guy's my friend."

He spread his hands on his desk. "She's always so certain about right and wrong! It's amazing; her moral compass never wavers." He shook his head. "I'm telling you, sometimes I really don't think I'm good enough for her."

"No kidding," Evie mumbled.

Vishal leaned back in his chair and tented his fingers. "Just imagine how impressed Abby would be to know that you played a pivotal role in saving Marvin." He looked up at the ceiling. "She would probably even call you a hero."

Gideon brightened. "Do you really think so?"

"Oh, definitely." Vishal nodded vehemently. "If you showed her that you *really* care about animals, I bet she would totally stop being mad about the zoo. And if Marvin is found, I'm sure you could convince your friend Tommy to drop the whole B-17 thing." He put his hands behind his head. "It's pretty much a win-win."

Vishal could see his words turning over in Gideon's mind. The businessman rubbed his chin, mulling it over. "I bet Abby *would* think it was pretty romantic if I swooped in and saved the day." A small smile played across his lips. "I can just see it now, me coming out of the caves cradling that little red panda, and Abby crying tears of gratitude for my incredible act of heroism and self-sacrifice."

The twins raised their eyebrows at each other. There was no way either of them could see that happening, but they weren't going to tell Gideon that. "Oh, totally!" Zach said with forced enthusiasm. "You're so right!"

If he caught their sarcasm, Gideon didn't show it. "Okay, I'll do it," he said. "What should I wear?"

\*\*\*

The swing dance party was already well underway when Gideon and the kids arrived at the Wabasha Street Caves. The band onstage played a peppy tune as folks dressed in vintage clothing and elaborate hairdos artfully flung one another into the air and twisted back together again. The dance floor was bright with swirling skirts of every pattern and color of the rainbow. With his pinstriped zoot suit and gray fedora, Gideon blended in perfectly with the crowd. He straightened the monogrammed pink pocket square in his jacket, and the ruby-red heart pinned to his right sleeve flashed under the golden lights of the lobby. His face fell when he saw the four teens leaning against the wall in a shadowy corner. "What the heck are you supposed to be?"

"We still think Dr. Chang might be behind the kidnapping, so we went undercover in case he's here," Vishal said. His spiky hair had been smoothed flat and slicked straight back. It gleamed like patent leather. With his dark suit and tie, he looked like he worked at a funeral home.

"What did you use in your hair?" Evie asked. "It looks . . . sticky."

"Don't ask," Vishal said. "And whatever you do, don't touch it." He nudged Zach and Evie with his elbows. "Nice threads."

Zach was dressed in a white sailor suit with a matching cap set at a rakish angle, and Evie wore a gold-sequined flapper dress with her twist-outs pinned up under a gold satin cloche hat. "They're the costumes from our tap-dancing recital last year."

Vishal grinned. "Oh, trust me. I remember."

"And what about you?" Gideon asked Sophia.

"Well, Dr. Chang knows me the best, so I couldn't take any chances. My disguise is perfect, if I do say so myself." Sophia patted her long red wig and batted her eyes behind rhinestone-studded glasses. Her outfit was a crazy mishmash of party clothes from the fifties, sixties, and seventies.

"You look like the Little Mermaid fell into a thrift store reject bin," Vishal said.

"Exactly," Sophia answered. "Anyone who's ever met me knows I wouldn't be caught dead in this getup. My fashion sense is impeccable."

"Whatever," Gideon said. "I told Abby to meet me here at eight, so we need to hurry up and rescue that panda before she arrives. I need her to see me saving the day." He peered into the dance hall. "What do I have to do?"

"Just act normal and wait for someone to contact you," Evie said. "We'll be watching nearby. And if someone leads you away, make sure it's noticeable so we can follow you."

Gideon nodded and walked into the dance hall, and the kids followed a few moments later, keeping a safe distance. Gideon sidled up to the bar, making sure his heart pin was easily visible. His eyes slowly scanned the room.

Sophia, Vishal, and the twins noticed a few teens standing in a group, and they edged into the fringes, hoping to blend in. Suddenly the band started playing a new song and the group flocked onto the dance floor, leaving the four exposed. "What do we do?" Evie asked.

Sophia grabbed Vishal's hand. "We dance."

Evie stopped her. "Hold up. I'm not dancing with my own brother." She tapped Vishal. "Come on, Vish." Vishal followed her onto the floor.

Zach and Sophia looked at each other. In her heels Sophia towered over Zach, who was already small and slight for his age. "I guess we're doing this," Zach said. "Do you know how to swing dance?"

"Not really. I take ballet," Sophia said. Her voice was distracted as she searched the room, hunting for Marvin's kidnappers. Gideon still stood alone at the bar. "But how hard can it be?" A nearby girl sailed into the air as her partner flipped her. "Oh," Sophia said.

"Come on," Zach said. "We can just do the basic step." He showed her how to move her feet. "And don't forget to smile. We're supposed to be having fun, so stop looking like you're casing the place."

The four danced across the room with smiles plastered on their faces, their eyes darting through the crowded club in search of anyone who might try to contact Gideon. "Still no sign of Dr. Chang," Sophia said softly. In fact she didn't notice anyone familiar.

After they made a few circuits of the dance floor, Zach stood on tiptoe to whisper in Sophia's ear. "Are you seeing what I'm seeing?"

# CHAPTER
## 22

"Gideon's not the only one with a heart pinned to his sleeve," Zach whispered. "What do you think it means?"

"I don't know, but look," Sophia whispered back. "The people with the hearts are disappearing from the room. Do you think they're the kidnappers? Why are there so many of them?" They danced over to Evie and Vishal and told them what they had noticed.

"Where's Gideon?" Evie asked. His spot at the bar was empty. "Is he on the dance floor?" The distinctive gray felt hat was nowhere to be seen.

"He must have slipped out with the others," Zach said.

"Shoot," Sophia hissed. "He was supposed to give us some kind of sign he was leaving so we could follow him. Maybe he double-crossed us and decided to take Marvin for himself!"

"I don't think he'd do that," Zach said. "Would he?"

"I don't know, but whatever he's doing, we have to find him," Evie said. "Let's search the caves."

Zach folded his arms. "I don't think that's a good idea. We don't know where we're going. What if we get lost?" He pulled out his phone. "Now it's really time to call Detective Bermudez."

"Good luck with that," Sophia said. "We're underground, so if you want to get a signal, you're going to have to go outside." She started walking over to a doorway marked PRIVATE: GUIDED TOUR GROUPS ONLY. "And by the time you get back in, we'll be long gone." Evie and Vishal followed close behind her.

Zach stood still for a moment, paralyzed with indecision. When the door closed behind them, he gave in and rushed after them. "Why do they always do this to me?" he mumbled, yanking on the heavy door.

The caves were shadowy, lit only by the occasional bare bulb hanging at intervals overhead. Zach let his eyes adjust to the gloom. Technically the caves weren't real caves; they were caverns that had been carved deep into the cliffside by the silica miners who had bought the land back in the 1840s. The arched ceilings and dark doorways reminded Zach of the ancient underground aqueducts his family had visited on a trip to Rome. Or catacombs. He shivered.

He found the others lurking behind a rickety stack of wooden racks. "Any clue on where everybody went?" he whispered.

"Not yet," Evie whispered back. "Let's keep going." They passed through the larger, more well-lit caverns and into a section where the passages were smaller and darker. Evie pointed to a scorch mark on the cave's rough floor, with a matching mark overhead. "I remember this spot. Our tour guide told us that the squatters who were living in the back caves came out and lit a fire here, and that's why the stone is all black."

"Smugglers used to use the caves a lot, too," Vishal added. "There must be all kinds of secret entrances and exits so they could come and go without anyone seeing."

"That's right," Zach said softly. "The guide told us there even used to be a hidden nightclub around here called a speakeasy. Lots of gangsters used to hang out there. She didn't show us how to get inside, though."

"It must be around here somewhere," Vishal said, leading the way. He passed a pile of shallow wooden crates that sat outside a narrow passageway. "What are these doing here?"

"They used to grow mushrooms in the caves," Zach answered. "The crates were probably for shipping them."

Vishal pointed. "No, I meant inside the crates." Scattered in the top crate were paper fans with wooden handles. Each had a large red number printed on a white background. "I think they're fans, but why would they need fans back here? It always stays cold in caves."

Sophia leaned forward and peered inside. "I've seen those before, and I'm pretty sure they're not fans. We must be close, so everyone keep your voice down." She led the others down the passage where a wooden door stood slightly ajar. They peered through the crack in the door, and Sophia pressed her lips together for a moment. "Yup. It's exactly what I thought."

"They're auctioning off that brown spider monkey," Sophia breathed. "The kidnappers smuggle and sell endangered animals."

"Marvin must be one of them," Zach whispered. "But where is he?"

"He's got to be somewhere nearby," Vishal said. From inside the room there was the sound of polite applause, and a woman dripping with diamonds smiled triumphantly. One of the dark-suited men that stood near the front of the room picked up the monkey's cage and carried it off the stage and through a side door.

"You can collect your item at the end of the auction after you've paid the cashier," the auctioneer said. "And for our next item, we have this Tibetan mastiff puppy, a direct descendant of the prizewinning Big Splash. We will start the bidding at three-hundred thousand."

"Three-hundred thousand?" Evie hissed. "You could buy a house for that!" Two of the black-suited men carried in a crate with a puppy inside. The puppy was big and fluffy, but it was shivering in the corner, curling its body against the wire mesh walls. The men set the crate down on the stage.

"Didn't one of those dogs go missing recently?" Vishal asked. "We saw a flyer for it at the police station."

"It's got to be the same dog," Zach answered.

"Wow. Endangered animals *and* stolen pets; these guys are real winners," Evie whispered sarcastically. The puppy started crying, and Evie's hands tightened into fists. "So how do we stop them? We can't just burst in there. There's way more of them than us, and they might be armed."

"I don't know," Sophia said. "Our plan was based around Gideon meeting the kidnappers alone so we could follow them to find Marvin. We weren't planning for an auction."

"I knew we should have called Detective Bermudez," Zach said.

Just then, three of the bidders stood up and threw down their paddles. "Everybody freeze! This is a raid! You are all under arrest for the sale and trafficking of endangered species and stolen property!" The undercover agents pulled out their badges, and uniformed officers burst through another side door. People screamed as everyone in the room scrambled in different directions. A few panicked bidders came tearing toward the door, and the kids ducked out of the way as it slammed open.

"Should we try to stop them?" Evie cried as a well-dressed couple ran past her.

"No time! We have to stay focused," Vishal answered. Inside the room the agents were wrestling their way through a throng of escaping bidders and men in dark suits, collaring whomever they could catch. Vishal pointed to the far corner of the room, where the auctioneer was slipping out through a small opening in the wall. "He looks like the guy in charge. Let's follow him!" Before anyone could respond, Vishal ran across the room and darted through the doorway. Evie and the others squirmed through the melee and raced to catch up.

They trailed the man, who disappeared around the corner of a long, twisting passageway. "Down there!" Zach cried. They streaked around the corner and followed the tunnel as it twisted and turned deeper underground.

Finally, they rounded the last bend and stopped in their tracks, stunned. The passage was a dead end. "Where did he go?" Zach asked. A small mountain of junk was piled against the wall, but there was nowhere to hide. "Did we miss a turnoff?"

"No," Vishal said. "I checked as we ran. There were no breaks in the walls anywhere!"

"Well, he has to be *somewhere*," Sophia said. "He can't have just disappeared."

"Yeah, but *where*?" Zach kicked at the pile of clutter. "There's no place to hide in this junk."

Evie grabbed his arm. "Or is there?"

# CHAPTER
## 24

Evie pointed to the door that was hidden in the wall behind the junk.

"Are you kidding me?" Vishal asked. "Seriously, how many secret lairs are there in this city?"

Zach pointed to the bar of blackness at the bottom of the door. "There's no light showing. He could be waiting in the dark to ambush us."

"Us?" Sophia scoffed. "I doubt it. He's on the run from the cops. I hardly think he's going to bother lying in wait for a few kids that he doesn't even know are chasing him."

"Still, he might've heard us running down the passageway," Zach said, lowering his voice. "We need to make him drop his guard so he won't think we were following him." He pulled a mini flashlight out of his pocket, winked at the others, and raised his voice almost to a shout. "Hey, guys! I think this is the spot where I lost my retainer on our school trip earlier." He clicked on the flashlight. "Will you help me look for it?"

"Oh, get real," Evie said. "Nobody is going to think you lost your retainer behind a *secret door*." She activated the flashlight on her phone. "What made you decide to come up with that? You don't even wear a retainer."

"Shhh!" Zach pointed to the door. "*He* doesn't know that," he whispered. He raised his voice to a shout again. "Hey, look! Maybe it's behind this door!" Evie rolled her eyes, and Zach put his hand on the doorknob. "You guys ready?" he whispered. The others nodded and tensed.

Zach threw the door open. "Wow, it sure is dark in here," he hollered. "Good thing we brought flashlights. My retainer must be around here somewhere." The kids crept forward, but no one sprang out at them.

There was a rustling noise from the far side of the room. "What was that?" Vishal cried. He swung his flashlight beam toward the sound, but all that reflected back was a pair of glowing green eyes. Vishal shrieked. "There's something over there!" Suddenly the room was flooded with light, and three of the detectives jumped, their eyes darting every which way.

"Oh, relax," Sophia said. "All I did was turn on the lights." She walked into the center of the empty room and looked around. "Whoever was here is gone now."

"Then whose eyes did I see?" Vishal challenged.

"Theirs," Sophia said, her voice suddenly quiet. She pointed at the cages lined up along a wall of shelves. The animals inside them blinked at the bright light, and a spotted Bengal cat meowed and pawed at the mesh of her crate. Next to her, two lemurs were crammed into a cage that was much too small for them. They clung to each other.

"This is awful," Evie said. "Those poor animals!" She walked over and began searching the shelves. "Where's Marvin?" Her foot accidentally kicked a bag of kibble on the floor, and a mouse scurried out of a hole near the top. She jumped back and looked at the label on the bag. "Does that label say *leaf* eater biscuit?"

Sophia nodded. "We have it at the zoo. A lot of the monkeys eat it."

"Zoo food," Vishal said thoughtfully. "So that could mean that Dr. Chang *is* behind this. I mean, just that Tibetan mastiff alone would probably cover the zoo's shortage of funds, plus give him a little extra for himself."

"No way," Sophia said. "These animals are in terrible condition. Dr. Chang would never allow that, not even if it was to save the zoo. I know him. He loves animals. There's no way he's behind this."

"Are you sure?" Vishal asked. "You've been wrong before."

Sophia shook her head firmly. "Not about this." Tears pooled in the corners of her eyes. "No one who loves animals could see this and not be absolutely horrified." She blinked the tears away. "Let's keep moving. We have to find Marvin."

"But how can we? We don't even know if he was ever here," Zach said.

Sophia pointed to a large plastic tub on the floor.

"Oh, he was here all right." She pulled a stalk of bamboo from the plastic tub. "Ninety-five percent of a red panda's diet is bamboo. And it looks like that auctioneer took a bunch with him when he came through here. He must have grabbed Marvin, too."

Evie ran to the other side of the room and swung open the door. "We've got to hurry, then. Come on!"

"What about the other animals?" Zach asked.

"Leave the doors open and the lights on; the cops will find them," Evie called back. "We can't lose Marvin!" The others followed her down another dimly lit passageway, and a few moments later they found themselves outside again, standing at the tree-covered mouth of a cave that looked down onto the open water of the nearby river.

Below them was a bustling riverfront. Trucks and cars were parked tightly together in the gravel lot, and boats of all sizes were moored to the jetty. It was evening, but the dock was busy with returning fishermen, pleasure cruisers, and local shippers loading up deliveries. The detectives saw crates, carriers, coolers, and picnic baskets everywhere they looked. "Oh, no!"

Sophia moaned. "We're never going to find him. He could be anywhere!"

A few moments later, Evie let out a triumphant cry. "I found him!"

"There!" Evie pointed. "On the deck of the *Purloined Letter*!" The four detectives ran down the hill and paused behind a white van.

"Now what?" Zach asked.

"There's no one on the boat's deck, so I say we hop on, grab Marvin's carrier, and take off." Vishal looked at the others. "What do you think?"

Zach thought a moment. "It's doable, but we'll have to be quick. And we can't act suspicious."

"Works for me, as long as you don't try to act like you lost your retainer again," Evie said. "That's got to be the worst cover story you've ever come up with!"

"I was under pressure," Zach said defensively. "It was all I could think of!"

"Look," Vishal said, "the kidnappers haven't seen us yet, so we just need to act like normal kids. There are tons of families with boats. Let's just act like we're one of them."

"Fine, whatever, now hurry up! They could have sailed to China by now while you all sat around and debated. Let's *go!*" Sophia grabbed Evie's wrist and pulled her through the parking lot. The boys followed.

Zach tried for a relaxed smile, but he could feel his lips stretching wide like the mouth of a jack-o'-lantern. "Act casual, act casual, act casual," he whispered to himself, trying to relax. He rolled his shoulders.

"Dude, why are you talking to yourself?" Vishal asked.

"I'm not!" Zach said quickly.

"Yeah, no, you definitely were," Vishal replied. "And why are you making that weird face? You look like the grimace emoji."

"Sorry!" Zach answered. "I'm just nervous."

"Don't be!" Vishal patted his friend's shoulder. "We got this, okay? It's a piece of cake. We just hop on and hop off, no big deal. And besides, there's like a million people around. We'll be fine."

"Okay," Zach said, trying to relax his muscles and match his friend's easy gait. "Piece of cake," he whispered to himself. "It's a piece of cake. Hop on, hop off. Pieeeece of cake."

"Dude, you're whispering to yourself again!"

"No, I'm not! I was just . . . I'm just singing a little song, you know, like people do when they're relaxed and everything's normal." Zach hummed tunelessly, watching for Vishal's reaction out of the corner of his eye.

Vishal grinned and shook his head. "Whatever, dude. Just try not to have a heart attack or something, okay?"

*Heart attack. Great. Something new to worry about.* Zach hummed louder.

When they reached the *Purloined Letter*, the deck was still empty. Most of the people on that section of the dock were gone, and the ones that remained were rough-faced watermen who looked like they kept to themselves. They tied their boats off quickly and expertly, keeping their eyes on their work.

Vishal took one final glance around before hopping

casually on board. Even in his dress shoes, he made almost no sound when he landed. *How does he do that?* Zach wondered. Evie hopped in after him, and Sophia followed, stumbling a bit in her kitten heels. Zach was last, and the leather soles of his dress shoes skidded a bit on the slick surface of the deck when he landed. He flapped his arms wildly and let out a piercing "Gaaah!" like a bird that had been suddenly yanked downward by its legs. His sailor hat slipped over one eye, and he barely managed to right himself in time to keep from tumbling off the boat.

"Very smooth," his sister noted. "You really stuck the landing."

Zach chose to ignore her. "Let's grab Marvin and get out of here." The red panda was huddled up in his carrier, his ringed tail twined around his feet. He sniffed at them suspiciously through the wire mesh door. "It looks like he's scared, but okay," Zach said. His hand curled around the carrier's handle, but before he could pick it up, Sophia stopped him.

"Wait. We have to search the boat. If we take Marvin and leave, the kidnappers will get away, and we'll never know their identities. Then what's to stop them from doing this again?"

Zach gripped the carrier more tightly. "That's not what we talked about. We need to get off this boat. Now."

Sophia's eyes were pleading. "Zach, there could be other animals here. Animals that will end up who knows where if we don't find them. I wasn't kidding when I said that the illegal wildlife market is deadly. These guys in Indonesia tried to sneak cockatoos through customs by cramming them into empty *water bottles*. Almost half of them died."

"Yeah, but we could die, too, if somebody catches us on this boat!" Zach's voice was urgent. "Sophia, we have to *go*!"

"Fine. Then go without me." Sophia turned away and began methodically searching through the crates on deck.

"Sophia, come on. We're not going to leave you here alone," Evie said. "It will take you forever to finish searching. They're gonna come back and find you way before that."

Sophia pointed to the ladder that led to the hold below. "Well then, make yourselves useful and help me."

Vishal started climbing down the ladder. Zach grabbed his arm. "What are you doing? Let's go!"

"Dude, you know Sophia. She's not gonna leave this boat, and there's no way we're leaving her here alone." His head disappeared below the hatch as he hopped down into the galley. His voice floated up to the deck above. "The faster we search, the sooner we get out of here."

Evie pushed past Zach to join Vishal. "Have you found anything yet?" she called down.

"Not yet," Vishal answered, and Evie scrambled down the ladder to join him. Zach stood there helplessly as he watched her go. He took another glance down the empty dock and started searching the deck.

A short time later, Zach heard an excited squeal from the hold. "Guys! We found something!" Evie cried.

"Then grab it and let's go," Zach called back. Vishal and Evie tumbled out of the hatch, triumphant smiles on their faces. They held a piece of paper in their hands.

"We picked up a captain's license for someone

named Sergei Barkovich," Vishal said.

Evie scanned the deck. "Have you guys found any other animals on board?"

Sophia picked up Marvin's carrier. "No. I think Marvin's the only one here. We've got what we need, so let's get out of here."

Zach let out a huge sigh of relief. "Finally!" He grinned. "I was really starting to worry we might never make it off this boat!" But Zach's grin quickly faded when he looked down the dock. "Oh, no! Guys, they're coming!" The others stared in horror as they spotted the auctioneer walking briskly down the wooden dock, talking intensely into his cell phone as two burly men in dark suits trailed at his heels. Just behind them was a man with a dark beard and an eyepatch. His heavily tattooed forearms bulged beneath the rolled-up sleeves of his denim work shirt.

"Okay, don't panic," Vishal said quietly. "We just need to find a place to hide."

"Don't panic?!" Zach whispered fiercely. "How am I not supposed to panic?! That guy has an *eyepatch*! That's, like, Villains 101!" He ducked down and peeked over the edge of the boat. "They're gonna be here any second, and Eyepatch Guy is gonna make shark bait out of us!"

"Zach, this is the Mississippi River. There aren't any sharks," Sophia said. "Besides, I already spotted the perfect place for us to hide."

# CHAPTER
# 26

Sophia led the others over to the dinghy hooked to the back of the boat. "Quick! Climb in before they see us!" she instructed. They crammed in and pulled the tarp over themselves just before the smugglers reached the boat. Eyepatch Guy untied the moorings and climbed into the captain's chair while the others disappeared into the hold below. The thrum of the engine grew louder as the boat pulled out of the slip and picked up speed.

"Okay, we can assume that Eyepatch Guy is definitely Sergei, since he's driving the boat," Vishal said, the roar of the engine keeping his voice from carrying too far. "But who are the others? And where are they from? I wish it weren't so dark under here so that we could check out that captain's license."

"I'm sorry that the conditions of our hiding spot

don't meet your needs," Zach whispered sarcastically. "Isn't anyone else worried about where we're going or how to get out of here? We can't stay here forever, you know. What if we have to pee?" He grimaced. "Oh, great. Now that I said that, I have to pee."

"Every boat has to stop eventually, right?" Vishal said. "We'll just wait until the boat ties up for gas or something, and then sneak off." He lowered his voice. "And if you really have to go, just pee in your pants. I won't tell."

"Perfect," Zach muttered. "We'll all just stay under here peeing our pants until we get to New Orleans or wherever. Great plan, Vish."

"Wait a minute," Evie said. "We're in a dinghy, right? Why don't we just wait until they're asleep, cut the ropes and let the dingy drop into the water? They'll keep going, and it will be hours before they realize anything is wrong. In the meantime, we'll have Marvin." She felt around the tiny dinghy. "Where is Marvin, anyway?"

"I had to leave his carrier on deck," Sophia whispered back. Her voice was heavy with regret. "If they had seen he was missing, they would have searched the boat and we'd all be caught for sure."

Evie squeezed her friend gently. "Got it. Okay, we can regroup. Don't worry. We'll figure out how to get him back and find a way off this boat. No problem." Evie tried to sound calm and reassured. Inwardly, though, her heart was sinking. She had no idea where they were headed or when they might stop. She wished she knew anything at all about boats, but the only experience she could remember was riding the Staten Island Ferry on a family trip to New York City.

Beside her, Zach sighed quietly. "I wish Detective Bermudez were here. I should have called him when we had the chance."

Evie nudged him. "Zach, of course! That's it! Your phone! Take it out and call him now!"

Zach's voice was barely a whisper. "I can't. I lost it."

"You lost it? When?"

"I don't know, but I think I dropped it when I was pretending to look for my retainer."

Evie briefly closed her eyes and struggled to maintain her composure. After a moment, she spoke. "Does anyone else have Bermudez's number?"

Vishal sounded equally despondent. "My phone is dead."

"Dead? How?" Evie asked.

"I forgot to charge it," Vishal admitted.

Evie felt a headache coming on. "Sophia?" she asked.

"I didn't bring mine," Sophia answered.

"You didn't *bring* yours?" Evie repeated. "Sophia, you're practically glued to your phone. How did you not bring it?"

"I was undercover, remember?" Sophia said. "Sophia Boyd always has her phone, but Penelope Boodakian *hates* technology."

"And who is Penelope Boo—" Evie struggled to complete the last name.

"Boodakian."

"Right. Who is Penelope Boodakian, exactly?"

Sophia straightened the red wig she still wore and adjusted the rhinestone-studded glasses. "She was my undercover character. I made a whole backstory for her. Ask me anything about her."

"Really? Anything?" Vishal asked, intrigued. "Okay, how about—"

"Nope," Evie said. "Nope, nope, nope, nope, nope. Nobody is going to ask anything about Penelope Boo—whatever it is."

"Boodakian," Sophia corrected. "I named her after my tennis coach."

"Your real tennis coach, or Penelope's tennis coach?" Vishal asked.

"My real tennis coach," Sophia said. "He's really nice."

"If you two don't stop, I'm going to hurl you both into the water," Evie warned as she reached into her pocket. "Apparently I'm the only one with any sense in this entire boat," she hissed. "Seriously, we go undercover to track a group of dangerous animal smugglers and not one of you thinks to make sure you have a working phone?" She unlocked her phone with an angry slash. "Ugh. Of course there's no signal under here! Whatever. You don't need a signal to call 911. What's the name of the boat again?" She squirmed partially out from under the tarp and peeked down over the edge of the dinghy to read it. "Got it! The *Purloined Letter*." She quickly dialed the emergency number.

"Nine-one-one. Please state your emergency." Evie smirked at the others and held up the phone in triumph. She was just about to speak when the phone slipped from her hands and splashed into the river below. She watched the screen's faint glow fade into the murk as the phone sank and disappeared from view.

Nobody said anything for a while.

Finally, Zach's harsh whisper cut through the tense silence of the dinghy. "You guys, I still have to pee."

\*\*\*

No one spoke again until the boat's engine slowed and cut out. They could hear the men moving around the boat, calling to one another and tossing ropes. One of the kidnappers passed right by the dinghy, and the kids froze. "I tell you, if the gorilla gives me any trouble tonight, deal is off," the man called out in a heavy Russian accent. "This animal is not like the others. It has caused us nothing but trouble!" The other men grunted in agreement, and the voices faded as the men walked away.

Sophia gasped. "Oh, no! They have a gorilla?"

"Don't worry," Evie said. "We'll find a way to save it, too."

Off to one side they could hear another sound. The low, slow drone of an engine, and something else. It sounded like music, and people talking. A woman's loud laugh carried across the water.

"Is that a . . . party?" Sophia whispered. She lifted a tiny corner of the tarp and peered out before ducking her head back under. "It is! We're tied up to one of those party riverboats that people rent out for cruises. There's some kind of banner hanging off of it, but I can't read what it says. It looks like three of the guys are climbing up the ladder onto the other boat, but I'm not sure where Sergei is."

"Who?" Zach asked.

"Eyepatch Guy."

"Right."

"Listen, this is our chance to grab Marvin and escape," Vishal whispered. "We need to get ready so we can make our move after Sergei's gone. Does everyone have everything?"

"Wait a minute, escape to where?" Zach asked.

"Onto the party boat," Vishal answered. "We can find the captain and call for help."

"Um, but didn't Sophia say the bad guys are going onto the party boat?" Zach asked. "I'm pretty sure when people are escaping, they try to escape *away* from the bad guys."

"Look, there are a ton of people on that boat. We can blend in, and the bad guys won't even know we're there," Vishal said.

"Yeah, in case you haven't noticed, Evie and I are wearing tap-dancing costumes, and Sophia looks like she wandered out of someone's fever dream." Zach eyed Vishal critically. "But I guess you might be able to pass if the party happens to be a convention of child accountants."

"Fine. We'll just hop on the boat and duck into a side room before somebody sees us. Then we'll find the captain and call the cops."

"Have you considered the other boat's captain might be *in on it*? It's not like these guys tied up to the party boat in secret," Zach answered. "For all we know, that's a party boat filled with bad guys, and then instead of hiding from four bad guys, now we have to hide from a hundred of them."

"So you're saying it's a bad-guy party boat," Vishal said skeptically.

"What I'm saying is that we can't take that risk. We're still trapped."

"There is another idea," Evie said. The others looked at her. "We get Marvin, unhook the dinghy, and take off while they're gone."

"Evie, none of us knows anything about boats," Zach said.

"I do," Sophia said suddenly. "We have a boat at our lake house. My parents let me drive it all the time."

"But we don't know where we are," Zach said. "How are we going to know where to go?"

"We just steer toward any lights we see on the shoreline. With a small craft like this we don't have to worry about running aground. Where there are lights, there are people, right? We'll just follow the lights and go ashore for help."

The twins and Vishal nodded slowly. "I think this

could work," Zach said. "Okay, so we wait until Sergei's off the boat, then we grab Marvin, and under the cover of darkness we untie the dinghy and escape." A smile broke out on his face. "I like it. No bad guys. It's the perfect plan!"

The sound of footsteps moved across the deck, and the four kids held their breaths until the footsteps passed. A few moments later they heard Sergei climbing up the ladder. Sophia peeked out from the tarp and saw him disappearing into the boat's cabin with a metal briefcase in his hand. "Oh, a metal briefcase," she whispered. "I'll bet anything there's money in there. But for who?"

"No time to worry about that," Zach said. "Let's grab the carrier and get out of here before he comes back." He and the others slithered onto the deck. Vishal padded over to Marvin's carrier, but when he got there he stopped in his tracks.

"Come on, Vish!" Zach hissed. "Grab Marvin and let's move!"

"I can't," Vishal said.

# CHAPTER
## 27

"Why not? His carrier's right there."

Vishal swallowed thickly. "His carrier might be here, but Marvin's gone."

The kids crowded around the empty carrier. "They must have taken him with them when they boarded the party boat," Sophia whispered. "Why didn't I listen to Zach before? We should have just grabbed the carrier and taken off when we first found him. Marvin needed me, and I let him down." Tears slipped down her cheeks. "What was I *thinking*?"

"You were thinking about the other animals that could be in danger," Evie said. "If I were an animal, I sure would feel lucky to have you on my side."

"Really?" Sophia asked.

"Are you kidding?" Evie asked quietly. "Sophia, you're amazing! We never would have gotten this far without you."

"And besides, you heard the kidnappers. They were talking about a gorilla! You were totally right to keep looking," Zach added.

"Thanks," Sophia said, wiping her eyes.

"Don't worry," Vishal said. "We got your back. That's what friends do, okay? We're all gonna get home safe, including Marvin *and* the gorilla."

"Definitely," Evie said. She peered across the dark water. "I'm still not sure where we are, exactly, but I'm glad we're all here together, at least."

"Me too," Zach said. "Cool. I'm psyched we're doing this. Everything's fine and super-great." He shoved his hands into the pockets of his sailor pants. "So, what are we supposed to do now?"

"We follow them," Vishal answered. He leaped onto the rope ladder and started climbing.

Zach grabbed his arm. "Vish, wait! We don't know what we're getting into. Boarding that riverboat is too big a risk!"

"It's a risk we have to take," Vishal said. "We're here to rescue Marvin. And one way or another, we're gonna rescue him. Come on, Penelope!" He continued up the ladder, and Sophia followed.

Evie climbed up onto the deck of the riverboat with Vishal and Sophia. Zach bit his lip in indecision for a moment before clambering up after them.

The rear deck was empty, but it was set up for dining. Large, round tables, each covered in a white tablecloth, still bore the remnants of an earlier dinner. Most of the plates had been cleared, but a few china dessert plates remained along with half-empty glasses.

"Chip chip and cheerio, mates, shall we search the boat, then?" Sophia asked.

"Why are you talking like that?" Evie asked.

"I'm undercover again," Sophia explained. "Penelope has an Armenian father and a British mother. She grew up in London. Do you want to know what her favorite food is?"

"No," Evie answered. "Listen, Marvin's kidnappers must be on this boat to meet someone. Maybe even more than one person. And unless this really is a bad-guy party boat, they probably won't want to meet in public. Be on the lookout for any closed cabin doors, tucked-away spots, anywhere someone could have a secret meeting."

"What if they finish the meeting and get away before we find them?" Zach asked.

"I'll take care of that," Vishal answered. He pulled a pocketknife out of his jacket and started sawing on the ropes that moored the *Purloined Letter* to the riverboat.

"Wait a minute, you've had a pocketknife the whole time and you didn't tell us?" Zach asked in a hurt voice.

"Why would I tell you that I had a pocketknife?" Vishal asked.

"I don't know; we might have needed one."

"Well if we'd needed a knife, I would have told you that I had one." Vishal finished cutting through the first rope. "You know, like I did just now."

"Well, still," Zach said. "Maybe if I'd known you had a pocketknife with you earlier, I could have used it to come up with a plan."

"Really, Zach? What would the plan have been? Take the kidnappers out one by one like a commando?"

Vishal cut through the second line, and the *Purloined Letter* slowly began to drift away down the river.

"Gross! No," Zach said. "Just, you know, in case we had to unlock something, or the bad guys put us in a bag and threw us into the river and we had to cut our way out."

"So, like, if we were Houdini?" Vishal folded his knife and put it back into his pocket.

Zach threw up his hands. "Look, all I'm saying is, you know, maybe next time we're in a situation like this and you have a valuable resource like a pocketknife, you could remember to tell the other people on your team."

"You got it, dude," Vishal said, patting his friend on the back. "The next time we're trapped on a boat with animal smugglers, I promise I will tell you right away if I have my pocketknife."

The sounds of the party grew louder as a door opened. "Someone's coming!" Evie whispered. "Hide!" They dropped to the deck and crawled under one of the cloth-covered dining tables.

"Man, I hate working these stupid fund-raisers," a male voice said. "Nobody ever tips." Glasses clinked as someone loaded them onto a tray.

"Tell me about it," a female voice answered. "But at least it beats those college graduation cruises. I've cleaned up enough puke on those things to last a lifetime!" Underneath the table Sophia made a disgusted face. The servers disappeared back inside, and the door to the party closed again.

Evie popped back up. "Okay, let's go!" She pointed at a set of stairs. "We'll start upstairs. More private space up there where they could be meeting." They hurried up the stairs and paused in the narrow hallway at the top. "Listen at the doors, but don't open any of them. We don't want the smugglers to know we're looking for them." Three of the detectives started down the hallway, but a fourth lingered behind.

"Dude, let's go! What are you waiting for?" Vishal whispered.

"There's a bathroom right here, and I still really have to pee," Zach whispered back.

"Fine. We'll wait for you outside the door."

"No, that's okay, just keep going," Zach said, shooing Vishal back down the hall.

"I don't think we should split up. I'll just call the girls back and we'll wait right here outside the door."

"Seriously, Vish. It's no big deal. I'll catch up in a sec, okay?"

"Not okay," Vishal answered. "What's the problem?"

Zach lowered his voice. "Come on, man. You know I'm a shy pee-er. If I think the girls can hear me, I won't be able to go."

"Dude, you and Evie share a bathroom. She's heard you pee like a million times."

"Yeah, but this is different. Sophia's here."

Vishal's eyes widened. "Oh, my god, do you like Sophia?"

Zach rolled his eyes. "No! Jeez, I don't have to *like* someone to want a little privacy." He pushed Vishal gently down the hall. "Look, I'm about to burst here, so just keep going, and try to stay out of sight. I'll catch up to you in a sec."

Vishal joined the girls, and Zach shut himself in the bathroom. "Finally," he groaned. "Whoo! That was a close call." He leaned his head against the wall and closed his eyes, certain that he had never peed so much in his entire life. The smooth surface of the wall felt cool against his cheek, and he let out a deep sigh of sweet relief. He could hear murmuring through the wall, and a man's laughter. The party must have carried upstairs.

Suddenly the voices sharpened and got louder. "What do you mean you have it with you? Are you crazy? You were supposed to sell that thing! Do you realize how much trouble you could bring down on our heads if it's found on this boat?" The voice was familiar, but Zach couldn't place it.

"Why did you not tell us this animal was famous? It is all over news! We cannot sell here. We tried. Nobody will buy! So we bring it here to you." Zach recognized Sergei's voice immediately.

"And just what the hell am I supposed to do with it?" the other voice said.

"Not my concern. Is your problem now." Sergei slammed something down on a table. "But we are businessmen and deal is deal. Here is your cut of profit for other animals." Zach heard something click open. He figured it must be the metal briefcase; Sophia said they always had money in them. "We give you twenty percent."

"Wait a minute, that wasn't what we agreed on! You said thirty percent!"

"You bring us much trouble with this creature. Police raided caves and arrested Dmitri and Maximilian. We had to leave animals behind." There was a long pause. "Even Tibetan mastiff." The briefcase closed, and when Sergei spoke again, his voice was smooth. "I think twenty percent from now on, yes? Twenty percent is more than generous." His voice grew ominous. "Unless you no longer wish to be in business?"

The other speaker cleared his throat nervously. "No, no, you're right. Twenty percent is fine."

"I thought so," Sergei answered. Zach heard the door open, and he prayed Vishal and the girls weren't still in the hallway. He heard footsteps retreat down the back stairs, but he waited until it had been quiet for several minutes before he opened the bathroom door and hurried farther down the hall.

A door opened next to him, and Zach let out a scream.

"Relax, it's us," Evie said.

"I thought we agreed we wouldn't go into any rooms," Zach said reproachfully.

"We heard someone coming, and we needed a place to hide."

"Then why did you open the door when you heard me walk by? I could have been the bad guys!"

Evie snorted. "Oh, please. You think I wouldn't recognize my own brother's walk?"

Zach's voice softened. "Aww, you recognized my walk?"

"Of course I did. You'd recognize mine, wouldn't you?"

Zach rubbed his chin. "I don't know; I've never thought about it."

Sophia shoved past the twins into the hallway. "This family reunion is very touching, but can we please get back to searching the boat?"

"We don't have to anymore. I heard the whole entire deal go down!" Zach filled the others in on everything he heard. "Whoever was meeting with Sergei has Marvin and the money." He frowned. "But whoever it was didn't *want* Marvin." He shook his head. "It doesn't make sense. Sergei complained that Marvin was too famous to sell. So why have Marvin stolen if nobody will buy him?"

"Maybe the guy didn't know that. Maybe he thought Marvin would sell at a higher price *because* he's so well-known," Evie suggested.

"It didn't seem like that," Zach said. "It was almost like the guy didn't even care whether Marvin was sold or not."

"What about the gorilla? Did anyone mention that?" Sophia asked.

"No," Zach answered.

"Did you see the guy's face?" Sophia asked. "Could you describe him to cops?"

Zach shook his head. "I was in the bathroom, remember? I didn't see anyone." He looked up at the ceiling, thinking. "But I know I recognized the voice from somewhere. I'm certain it's someone I've met before." He grunted in frustration. "But I can't remember *where*."

Sophia took Zach by the shoulders and steered

him toward the main staircase at the front of the boat. "Let's head down to the party and see if we can jog your memory."

The group took a moment to tidy up before they walked into the party. The glass doors were frosted, but the movements inside were glittery enough that they could tell it was fancy. Evie straightened her hat, and Sophia pulled off a few accessories and shoved them behind a plant. Vishal did his best to smooth down his hair, which had begun to stand up in several different places. Zach looked down at his sailor suit and sighed. "What am I supposed to do?"

"Take off the hat, maybe?" Sophia plucked it off his head. "And here. Wear this." She pulled off Vishal's jacket and helped Zach into it. The shoulders slumped, and the sleeves hung well below Zach's hands. "Never mind," Sophia said. "You look like a sad scarecrow." She handed Vishal back his jacket and put Zach's hat back on his head. "I say go with the sailor-boy thing. Maybe everyone will just think you work on the boat."

They pushed open the glass doors and entered the throng of people. "Remember, Sergei's contact was definitely a man, so don't waste time trying to recognize women," Evie said. "Try to remember everything you can about where you heard that voice."

"I am," Zach said. He scanned the room and tried to find someone he recognized, but the room was a sea of silver-haired men. "It's hard when they're all in tuxedos. Look at them! They might as well all be the same man!"

"Let's walk around, try to get a closer look," Evie suggested. The group cruised the perimeter. As they reached the far side of the room, someone stepped backward and bumped into them.

"Oh, excuse me!" The man turned around, and Sophia let out a gasp of dismay.

It was Darwin Chang.

***

"Oh, Sophia, I didn't know you were here," Dr. Chang said with a smile. His expression changed to confusion. "Why are you wearing a wig?"

Sophia stared at him speechlessly, her jaw hanging open. Her skin was as white as cheese, and she looked like she was about to throw up.

Vishal stepped in front of Sophia and smiled brightly. "It's for a school project," he explained.

Darwin's face relaxed, and he gave a nod of understanding. "Ah, of course," he said. "I see." He stretched his neck and looked around the room. "Where are your parents? I haven't seen them."

Sophia finally found her voice. Her horror turned to anger, and she could hear her blood pounding in her ears. "*How could you?*" She spat out each word as if it were poison.

Zach plucked at Sophia's sleeve. "Sophia!" She shook him off.

"You're supposed to love animals. You're supposed to take *care* of them!"

Dr. Chang stared at her, and a slow comprehension spread across his face. "I think I understand what this is about. But I can explain. It's all in the name of helping the zoo."

"Sophia!" Zach said again. "Listen to me!"

But Sophia was too angry to hear. "Is that what

you call it? Helping the zoo?" She shook her head. "Everyone said I was wrong, but I stuck up for you anyway!" She clenched her hand into a fist, and tears streamed down her face. "I believed in you!"

Zach grabbed Sophia and turned her around to face him. "Sophia! That's not the voice! It's not him!"

Sophia stared at him, uncomprehending for a moment. Then she blinked her eyes as if she had just come out of a trance. "What? It's not?"

"No," Zach said. "It's not."

"But didn't Dr. Chang just confess?" Sophia asked.

"He did, but I think it was for something else," Vishal said.

"Well, what was it, then?" She narrowed her eyes. "What did you do?"

Dr. Chang put out his hands in a placating gesture. "I understand that you are very upset right now. A lot of people are. B-17 is a cherished part of our city. But I think if we can work together, we can find a solution that's best for everyone. That's why I'm here tonight."

That's when Sophia really looked at where she was. She had been so busy focusing on faces that she hadn't noticed the rest of the room. "Of course," she whispered. "The gorilla."

"The gorilla?" Evie asked.

"The gorilla," Sophia answered. "I know who has Marvin."

Big Tommy Brown strode onto the stage and pulled the microphone out of the stand. It squealed in protest, and there was a burst of jolly laughter. "Sorry about that, folks!" Tommy pulled out a handkerchief and mopped his wet face. "Thank you all for joining me tonight as we celebrate my campaign for mayor. And thank you especially for all the generous donations I know you're going to make tonight!" Another burst of jolly laughter came from the audience.

Sophia pulled her friends away from Dr. Chang. "It's Big Tommy Brown, isn't it?" Sophia said softly. "Sergei wasn't talking about an actual gorilla; he was talking about Tommy. The Golden Gorilla Award. That's how he got his nickname."

Zach nodded. "That's the voice I heard with Sergei."

"But I don't get it," Evie said. "He's already getting a cut of all the animal smugglers' profits, right? So why did he want Marvin stolen so badly?"

Tommy paced the stage, working the crowd with jokes and folksy sayings. Then his voice dropped and grew serious. "Little Marvin was a symbol of our great Twin Cities. He was beloved by all. And mark my words, if I become mayor, I will not let his death be in vain. My opponent, our current mayor, did nothing to protect our city from the bloodthirsty predator that roams our streets. In fact, she wanted to host a festival celebrating this vicious killer! And while little Marvin was stolen from his bed and torn to pieces, what did our current mayor do? Why, she just sat back and did nothing. She may as well have given that bobcat a key to the city."

"That filthy liar," Sophia spat.

"Well, not on my watch," Tommy continued. "If I am elected, I guarantee that never again will vicious wildlife be able to take the lives of our precious zoo animals. Or our pets, like my beloved Peaches. Rest in peace. And certainly not our children!" There was roaring applause. "There are many city council members here this evening, and I hope you'll let them know that we're counting on their support as we work to make this city safe again."

"So that's why Marvin was stolen," Evie said bitterly. "To help his campaign."

"Create a problem, blame it on your predecessor; it's the oldest trick in the book," Zach said.

"Listen to everyone cheering for this garbage," Sophia said.

"Not for long, if we can help it," Zach answered. "Let's find Marvin and that briefcase so we can add a little surprise ending to Big Tommy's party."

Vishal gave his friend a sideways glance. "What?" Zach asked.

"Nothing," Vishal answered.

"It was that line, wasn't it?" Zach said. "I thought it sounded cool. Didn't it sound cool?"

"Sure," Vishal said noncommittally.

Zach's shoulders slumped. "It wasn't cool, was it?"

"Don't worry; you'll get there," Vishal reassured him.

"We're looking for a silver briefcase and some kind of bag or small animal carrier," Evie said. "Tommy was already in the room when we got down here, so it has to be close by. Spread out and look."

The group was just about to split up and search when Sophia felt a hand on her shoulder. "Sophia Elizabeth Boyd, *what* are you doing here?" Sophia looked up to see her parents, their expressions steely.

"Evelyn and Zachary Mamuya, I'd like to ask you the same thing." Evie and Zach cringed when they heard their mother's voice.

Vishal started to creep away when a hand grabbed the collar of his jacket. "Vishal Ramesh Desai, don't think you're going to slink away from this."

Vishal looked into his father's brown eyes and tried to smile. "We can explain."

Next to him Mrs. Desai's voice was ice. "Really? And what, pray tell, is your explanation for your presence at this event, to which you were most definitely not invited, and at which there are no other children?"

The four kids shrugged and looked at one another. "School project," they said in unison.

Their parents were unmoved.

"It's for a civics unit," Vishal said quickly. "Learning about how campaigns work and all that." He scanned the room. "In fact, our chaperone is probably looking for us. We should go find him!" He tried to dart away, but his father held his collar in a death grip.

"Wait a minute. Just what, exactly, are *you* doing here?" Sophia asked her parents. Her voice was hot and angry. "You know I've been working on the Wildlife Festival for months, and tonight you just stood there and applauded while Tommy Brown trashed it in front of everyone? You know what he's been saying about B-17. He wants to *kill* her. How could you still support him?" She turned to look at the other parents. "How could any of you?" She burst into tears and ran away.

The parents all stood, arms at their sides, stunned into silence. "Sophia, wait!" Evie and the boys ran after her.

They found her at the rear of the boat, staring out into the black water. "Are you okay?" Evie asked softly.

Sophia turned around. The tears were gone. "Oh, I'm fine. We just needed a way to get out of there, and Vishal certainly wasn't going to be able to pull it off."

"You sly dog," Evie said with a grin. "You are one heck of an actress, because I could have sworn you meant every word."

"Oh, I did," Sophia said. "I'm furious; I'm never speaking to my parents again." She pointed to the back staircase. "That's where they came down after the meeting, right? So I'm guessing Marvin and the money must be stashed back here, where it's quiet. That way if Marvin rustled around or made a bunch of noise or something, nobody would notice."

Zach crawled around on the deck on his hands and knees. "I don't see anything yet, do you?"

"Nothing over here," Vishal called.

"Keep looking," Sophia said. She ran her hands along the sides of the boat, searching for a secret compartment. "It's got to be here somewhere!"

Just then the back door opened and Sergei strode onto the deck. "Gorilla man's speech is almost over. Time to go." He walked to the edge of the deck, and when he looked down, he let out a cry of rage. "Where is boat?" he shouted.

"It should be right there," the auctioneer said. "Isn't it?"

Sergei grabbed him by the neck and forced his head down over the water. "Do you see boat?"

"I . . . I swear it was there when we left," the auctioneer stammered. "I tied it up myself!" He realized what he said and tried to back out of Sergei's grip. "I swear I tied it tightly. Somebody must have untied it. Or . . . or . . . look!" He pointed at the neatly tied knots that were still wrapped around the cleats, the ends cleanly severed. "Someone must have cut it loose!"

Sergei let out a roar of rage. He whirled around and pointed at Zach. "You! Sailor boy! Did you see anyone cut loose this boat?"

Zach froze in place. "Um . . . uh . . . n-n-no! I was, uh, working over on the, uh . . . the poop deck all night."

"A riverboat does not have a poop deck!" Sergei bellowed. He raised his fists and closed in on Zach. "You lie, sailor boy!"

Mr. and Mrs. Boyd burst through the back door, followed closely by the Desais and Mrs. Mamuya. Sergei dropped his fists and stepped back.

"Sophia!" Mareva cried. "Where have you been?

You can't just run off like that! We were worried sick!"

"Why was she worried?" Evie whispered to Vishal. "We're on a boat; it's not like there's anywhere she could go." Vishal snickered.

"I don't know what you have to laugh about, young man," Mrs. Desai said. "Unless you think being grounded for the rest of your life is funny." Suddenly she stopped and looked at Sergei and his henchmen, who were still standing menacingly over Zach. "Who are these men?"

Sergei jabbed a finger into Zach's face. "This sailor boy has cut ropes that hold my boat! Then he tells lies and cowers like dog! And now I will smash him like bug."

"Excuse me," Mrs. Mamuya said, stepping between Sergei and the children. "You're not smashing anyone, and certainly not my son." She set her jaw and held out her arms protectively. "Now kindly step away from the children and go back to your business."

The Russian turned on Mrs. Mamuya and jabbed his finger in her face. "*Nobody* tells Sergei what to do!"

"Uh-oh," Vishal whispered. "Did he just refer to himself in the third person? That can't be a good sign."

"Well, if *Sergei* is threatening to harm children, you better believe I'm telling *Sergei* what to do!" Mrs. Mamuya shot back. She stepped forward until they were eye to eye.

Vishal covered his mouth with his hand. "Whoa, Evie, your mom is mad fierce!"

Mr. Desai clapped sharply. "Vishal! Stop gaping and come over here this instant!"

The auctioneer grabbed Mrs. Mamuya's arm. "Ma'am, trust me, it's better if you let this go."

Mrs. Mamuya whirled at him, surprised. She shook her arm out of his grasp. "Don't touch me!"

"Sophia, what on earth is going on here?" Dashiell cried.

Sophia put her hands over her ears, closed her eyes, and let out the longest, loudest scream she had ever made in her life. *"Why can't everyone just leave me aloooooooooone?!"* She yanked open the door, winked at Evie, and ran inside.

"Sophia!" Evie shouted. "Wait! We can work this out!" The twins and Vishal tore down the hallway after

Sophia, the adults at their heels.

They burst back into the party, where Tommy was winding down his speech. His fleshy red cheeks glowed like two suns, and he had unbuttoned his collar and loosened his tie. As Sophia and her friends ran to the stage, they bumped into a familiar figure.

"Detective Bermudez!" Zach cried. "What are you doing here?"

"Extra security detail for the fund-raiser tonight," the detective said. "What about you? Is everything okay?" He looked at the stampede of angry adults behind them. "I'm guessing not. Wanna fill me in?"

"Too late for that now!" Sophia jumped onto the stage. "Just pay attention and try to keep up!" She walked over to Tommy and coolly took the microphone out of his hand. Tommy watched her, his blue eyes calculating.

"Let's give another round of applause to our beloved councilman, Big Tommy Brown!" Sophia said into the microphone. The audience cheered. "He is truly a man of the people, isn't he?" The audience cheered again.

"We planned a little special surprise for everyone to let Big Tommy know just exactly what he means to us." Sophia saw Tommy starting to relax. After all, he wouldn't have been able to stay in politics for this long if he hadn't learned to roll with the punches. Sophia passed the microphone to Vishal, and her eyes scanned the room. Where were Marvin and the money? They had to be here somewhere.

"Councilman Brown has had quite the successful career," Vishal said. "But did you know he's a successful businessman, too?" A group of silver-haired business-men let out loud whoops of approval. "He's been able to form wonderful business partnerships all over our Twin Cities," Vishal continued.

Tommy preened. "Building successful partnerships! That's what politics is all about!"

"I believe some of his business partners are here tonight. Isn't that right, Sergei?" Vishal asked. The Russian froze and stared daggers at Vishal. "In fact, Sergei gives a full thirty percent of all his illegal wildlife smuggling earnings to his old friend Tommy." There were a few gasps in the audience. Vishal smiled. "Oh,

I'm sorry. Twenty percent. You see, business had been going great for Sergei. Tommy was helping him find just the right animals to steal, and just the right buyers, and they were bringing in a lot of cash. He had even managed to secure a Tibetan mastiff—"

"My missing dog!" a woman in the audience cried.

"But then Tommy had to go and mess everything up by asking Sergei to steal the one animal he could never sell. An animal so famous and beloved that all of the Twin Cities knew him by name." He waited a beat. "Marvin." There were gasps of shock and confused murmurings from the crowd.

"All right, kids, your little prank has gone on long enough!" Tommy said with a chuckle. His face was jolly, but his eyes were steely and hard. He yanked the microphone out of Vishal's hand. "Everyone knows Marvin was killed by a bobcat, and no childish storytelling is going to change that. Now run along back to your parents."

"It's not wishful thinking!" Sophia shouted. "We *saw* him!"

Tommy turned off the microphone and walked over

to Bermudez, who was watching from the edge of the stage. "Hey, Pedro. You're part of my security detail, aren't you? So how about doing your job and getting these brats offstage?"

"The name's Peter," Bermudez said. "And I think everyone in the room would like to know what they have to say." He picked up a spare microphone and handed it to Zach.

"I guess that means you just tendered your resignation, because I'll make sure you never work in this town again," Tommy growled. "Or anywhere."

"B-17 is innocent!" Sophia shouted.

Tommy turned the microphone back on and grinned at the audience. "Looks like we have a few animal activists in the house tonight." He patted Sophia on the head condescendingly. "Ah, the idealism of youth. Let's see if you still want that bobcat around when your *own* pet goes missing."

"I bet your own pet isn't even missing," Sophia snapped. "I bet you faked it just to get people to feel sorry for you!"

Tommy turned off his mic and gripped Sophia by

the arm. "This isn't funny, kid," he said through his teeth. "Now get off the stage before I *make* you get off."

"Oh, trust me, there's nothing funny about it," Sophia shot back. "I'm as serious as a heart attack, which is probably exactly what you'll have as soon as we reveal to everyone in this room what a corrupt fraud you are!"

"Listen, sweetheart," Tommy said. "You already tried that, and guess what? Nobody's buying it. You know what they call it when you make false accusations in public? *Slander*. So unless you want to find your family in the middle of a lawsuit, I suggest you shut your mouth."

"Those accusations aren't false and you know it!"

"Nice try, kid. But without any evidence it's just your word against mine, and guess who everyone's gonna believe?" He snapped his fingers, and a group of men in dark suits pushed their way onto the stage, including Sergei's henchmen. He switched the mic back on. "Now if the rest of my security detail can please get these children off the stage, I think we'd all like to go home. Thank you all for coming. Good night."

The audience applauded, and Tommy switched off the microphone and put it back on the stand.

Sophia knew she had lost. "Whatever you do, just please don't hurt Marvin," she said. "At least promise me you'll find him a good home."

Tommy grinned at her and leaned close to whisper in her ear. "I wasn't planning to hurt the little guy, but after your stunt tonight, I'm going to put that panda in his little carrier, tie a rock to it, and drop him in the bottom of the Mississippi." He chucked her under the chin and walked off the stage.

One of the men in black grabbed Vishal by the elbow, and Vishal recognized him as one of Sergei's henchmen. "All right, kid. Let's go."

"What are you gonna do, arrest me?" Vishal asked.

"Oh, don't worry about that," the henchman said. "Where we're taking you, you won't have to worry about seeing the cops—or anyone else—ever again."

The security men crowded the stage, keeping the parents and Detective Bermudez away. "We just need to ask these children a few questions," one of the men said, "to make sure they don't pose a threat to the councilman, and then we'll release them into your custody."

Evie and Zach looked at each other in a panic. "Nobody believes us," Evie whispered. "He's gonna get away with it."

"Look at us," Zach whispered back. "He's a city councilman, and we're just four weird kids wearing dumb disguises. Would *you* believe us?"

Tommy was already back on the floor, shaking hands and slapping backs while his private security team surrounded the four detectives. The voices of the party grew louder.

Suddenly, Evie clutched Zach's hand. "Do you still have the microphone?"

"Yeah," Zach said.

"Give it to me!" Zach passed it over, and Evie switched it on. "Detective Bermudez!" Evie cried into it. "Marvin and the money are right here in this room!"

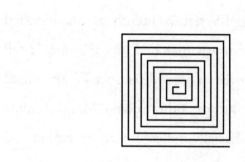

# CHAPTER
## 29

Evie watched the TV screen intently as a handcuffed Big Tommy Brown was marched out of court. "I tell you, I never get tired of a good perp walk." She raised her voice to call into the other room. "Mom? Tommy Brown just got officially indicted. Can we go out and celebrate?"

"No," her mother called back. "You're still grounded!"

"Come on, Mom," Zach said. "We caught a crooked politician and broke up an animal-smuggling ring. Surely that should be a mitigating factor?"

Mrs. Mamuya popped her head out of her office nook. "I swear you're going to grow up to be a lawyer."

"What about me?" Evie asked. "Can't I be a lawyer?"

"Not you," Mrs. Mamuya said. "You're going to be president."

"Does that mean we're not grounded anymore?" Evie asked.

"Even future presidents have to follow the rules," Mrs. Mamuya said. "You promised me you would never go on another case without telling me first, and you broke that promise. You could have gotten kidnapped, or even killed!"

"Plus we lost our phones," Zach added.

"Plus you lost your phones," Mrs. Mamuya echoed. "Which could also have gotten you killed. By me."

"Don't make it worse, Zach," Evie said. "Besides, at least I lost my phone doing something heroic. You lost yours acting out your dumb cover story that we didn't even need."

Mrs. Mamuya's phone rang. She answered it and handed it to Evie. "It's for you."

"Hey, Evie, it's me, Sophia."

"I know," Evie said. "It says it on the caller ID."

"Oh, good. Hey, can you and Zach come over for a little while? I already called Vishal, too."

"We can't. We're still grounded."

"So am I, but I asked my parents and they said it's okay as long as we don't leave the house."

"Let me check." Evie tucked the phone against her shoulder. "Mom, can we go over to Sophia's for a little while, as long as we promise to stay inside her house and not go anywhere? Her parents said it's okay."

"No. You're still grounded."

Evie put the phone back to her ear. "Nope. Still grounded."

"Too bad," Sophia said. "I was hoping we could celebrate Big Tommy's indictment together."

"Me, too," Evie admitted. "I hope they have enough to convict him. Detective Bermudez said that Sergei refuses to talk, and his men won't say anything, either. The cops know the smugglers are part of a much bigger network of criminals, but they're at a dead end."

"I hate thinking that we didn't get them all," Sophia said glumly. "Who knows how many animals are still out there suffering?"

"Don't worry, we won't give up. It looks like Marvin is the only animal that Bitsy stole, but Bermudez says they've gotten leads on the animals stolen by Sergei's smuggling ring. We'll find them all someday."

"Together?" Sophia asked.

"Of course together," Evie answered. "That's what best friends do."

\*\*\*

A few months later, a big banner was hanging across the zoo gates when the Mamuyas and the Desais arrived: WELCOME TO THE TWIN CITY WILDLIFE FESTIVAL. The zoo was crowded with visitors checking out booths on butterfly gardens, vermicomposting, and building bat houses. Many guests were wearing furry-eared headbands in honor of B-17, who had recently been voted the official mascot of the Twin Cities.

Evie waved to Sophia's parents, who broke away from their conversation with Gideon and Dr. Chang to welcome them. "Wow," she said. "This is amazing!"

"Everybody worked really hard to bring it together," Mareva said.

"Especially Sophia," Vishal said. "It's all she's been talking about for months. Where is she?"

"She's over in the MEOWS booth with Abby,"

Gideon answered. He pointed to a small tent nearby where his fiancée stood in front of a big educational display. He blew her a kiss, and Abby blew one back.

"Go on over and say hi," Dashiell added. "Soph'll be thrilled to see you!"

The kids found Sophia and Abby answering questions and passing out pamphlets. Zach stopped and grabbed Evie's arm. "Whoa. Is that who I think it is?"

Jersey Sinclair was also manning the MEOWS booth. She was crouched down with a group of toddlers, holding out a stuffed bobcat toy for them to touch. Abby reached down to hand her something, and the two of them shared a smile.

Sophia was chatting with a patron when she noticed Evie and the boys. She paused midsentence, and her face broke into a brilliant smile. "Excuse me," she said to the patron, "my best friends just arrived, and I need to go say hello." She waved wildly and then said something to Abby and Jersey. Jersey reached up to give her a hug before Sophia came over to join her friends.

Zach tapped Vishal on the arm. "Am I living in a

parallel universe, or did Jersey just *hug* Sophia?"

"Don't ask me, dude. I thought they were sworn enemies."

"You're here!" Sophia chirped. "What do you think of the festival?"

"Sophia," Evie said with feeling, "it's *incredible*! I can't believe you pulled this whole thing together!"

"Well, Abby and Jersey did most of it. They're both part of MEOWS now. And then when Dr. Chang got the zoo on board, everything really fell into place." She checked her watch. "I have about an hour break. Wanna go visit Marvin?"

"Definitely!" Zach said. "And maybe if we have time, we can stop by Shakti's exhibit, too?"

Sophia laughed. "Of course! We can't keep Zach away from his soulmate. Let me grab my bag and we'll go." She returned a few moments later with a look of confusion on her face and a package in her hands. It was wrapped in brown paper, and SOPHIA was written on the top in silver ink.

"What is that?" Vishal asked.

"I don't know. It was just sitting there with my name on it."

"Well, let's open it and see what's inside," Evie said.

The group found a quiet spot with a picnic table, and Sophia unwrapped the box. She slid off the lid and pulled out a stack of papers and ledgers. "What is all this?"

Evie opened up a ledger and slid her finger down the page. "Listen to this: pangolin, slow loris, hyacinth macaw. These are all endangered animals." She leafed through the pages. "And there are also names, bank account numbers, lists of financial transactions, everything." She looked up, beaming. "Zach, do you still have Bermudez on speed dial? Because I think we just found everything we need to take down the rest of Sergei's crime ring!"

Vishal whooped and high-fived Zach. "This is amazing, Sophia! Where did you get all this stuff?"

"I honestly don't know. It wasn't there when I put my bag under the table with the others. Things got pretty busy, then you guys showed up, and when I went to pick up my bag, the box was inside."

"Is there any note or anything?" Zach asked. "Any idea of who might have given it to you?"

"Just this." Sophia held up a blank manila envelope. She opened it up and slid out two smaller envelopes. One was thick and heavy, and it had FOR THE ZOO printed on the front. Sophia opened it and peeked inside. "Oh!" she cried.

"What is it?" Zach asked.

Sophia held open the envelope. It was stuffed with stacks of cash.

The other was an ordinary business envelope, addressed to the Gemini Detective Agency. Sophia pulled out the note that was folded inside.

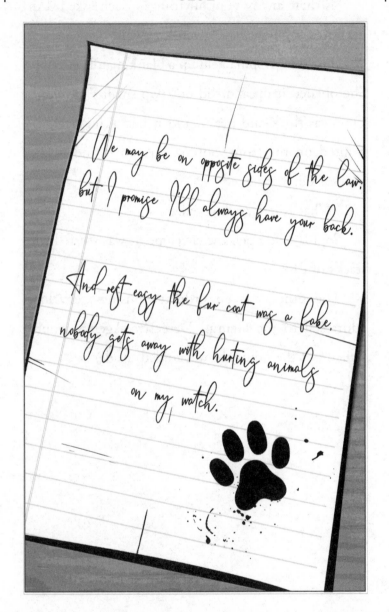

# Acknowledgments

This book is a work of fiction, but like all works of fiction, truth lies at the heart of it. As we keep expanding our reach into more and more wild spaces, plants and animals have had to work harder and harder to find ways to adapt to us. A classic example of this is P-22, a real-life mountain lion that makes his home in the eight square miles of Griffith Park, not far from the LA Zoo. P-22 is something of a legend in Los Angeles, and there is actually a festival there celebrating him each year. I extend my deepest thanks to the organizations that work to protect P-22 and other urban wildlife, especially Citizens for Los Angeles Wildlife (CLAW) and the National Wildlife Federation. I am also grateful to the research of Dr. Laurel Serieys and all the scientists who study and protect P-22 and others like him.

Poaching and the illegal wildlife trade are some of the biggest threats to plants and animals today, and we owe everything to groups that are fighting to stop it. There are too many to name here, but the International Union for Conservation of Nature (IUCN) and the World Wildlife Fund (WWF) are two you should know.

I am eternally indebted to the Los Angeles Zoo and Botanical Gardens, a place that became my second home when I lived in Los Angeles. Folks like Dani, Lauren, Jill, Nicki, Roxanne, Francisco, Crystal, Megan, Robin, and Patricia showed me the incredible level of thoughtful tenderness that keepers and zoos put into caring for animals. Thanks also to the docents at the LA Zoo and its training program, particularly Kirin Daugharty, Beth McClellan, Dillu Ashby, Norm Mitchell, Bill Mandel, and Landes Bell. James Ponti, Grayson Ponti, Tige Hutcheson, Michelle Benson, and Tom Ness all helped me find answers to my many questions about red pandas. They made sure I had every piece of information I could want, and any errors you find in the book are entirely my own. Both the Trevor Zoo and the National Zoo gave me opportunities to work with incredible animals back when I was a young college student, and those experiences are treasured ones.

My agent, Erin Murphy, and my extended EMLA family continue to inspire and delight, as does my wonderful team at Little Bee/Yellow Jacket. Huge thanks to Shimul Tolia, my editors Sonali Fry and Brett Duquette, my publicist Paul Crichton, and illustrators Kevin Hong and Damien Jones for putting so much love and enthusiasm into this series. It is a joy to work with you. And extra-fierce hugs to Erin Varley and Susan Sullivan for all of your support as readers, thinkers, and educators.

Writing books is hard, and I can never adequately express my gratitude to my friends and family for all of your support. I simply could not do this without your encouragement and loving acceptance. You are my habitat and my home, and I thank you all from the deepest depths of my wild, wild heart.